Tater's Crime

Sammy braced himself. "What was it like? That night. What was it like?"

Tater stared at him. Finally he said evenly, "It wasn't much."

Shivers skittered up and down Sammy's back like squirrels. "Wasn't you sorry? Or wished you could undo it?"

You had to be sorry, he thought. That's what the nightmares were.

Tater said, "Nix on that, Sammy. You can't undo it. Is that all you can think about?"

"Pretty near all."

"Well, don't. I don't."

"I wish you *did*. You ought to. You ought to be scared the law's going to come for you. Why didn't it, ever?"

"Hell, I don't know, Sammy. I can't let it bother me no more. I got to get on with my life. I can't wonder why about things."

I can't wonder either, Sammy warned himself. . . .

BANTAM BOOKS

TORONTO • NEW YORK • LONDON • SYDNEY • AUCKLAND

RL 5, IL age 11 and up

ON FIRE

A Bantam Book / published by arrangement with
Atlantic Monthly Press

PRINTING HISTORY
Atlantic Monthly Press edition published April 1985
Bantam edition / December 1987

The Starfire logo is a registered trademark of Bantam Books, Inc.
Registered in U.S. Patent and Trademark Office and elsewhere.

ISBN 0-553-26862-7

Published simultaneously in the United States and Canada

Bantam Books are published by Bantam Books, Inc. Its trademark,
consisting of the words "Bantam Books" and the portrayal of a rooster, is
Registered in U.S. Patent and Trademark Office and in other countries.
Marca Registrada. Bantam Books, Inc., 666 Fifth Avenue, New York,
New York 10103.

One

SAMMY HANEY HAD TO RAKE HIS HANDS along the bumpy ground to remember where he was. Even after eight days and nights on the road, it still surprised him to wake up under a black sky.

At his feet the fire had died. He bent his cold toes up and down inside his shoes, and sorted sounds to see which one had brought him awake. Coyote? A dog over toward town? His mother might have stirred in the wagon, covering one of the kids. His brother lay beside him, a long crescent as thin as a new moon, curled in his blanket to fit the grass humps. He was moaning again, but Sammy could block that off. He had learned to lie listening to the raw breaths, and jerks, and scared slurred talk without wondering what caused them. He didn't want to know.

A cottonwood branch popped. Someone, or something, was moving off up the slope from the creek, intent and angular. Sammy rose on his elbow for a better look, and sighed, recognizing what had nudged him out of sleep.

He touched his brother's shoulder. It cringed under the frosted blanket. "We got trouble," Sammy whispered. "Pap's leaving." A little rock clattered, farther up the slope. He waited. "Tater? You awake? Pap's took off for town."

"I can hear him thrashing around, good as you can," Tater said flatly, and turned away.

"Don't we even want to try to stop him?" An uneasiness bubbled up in him, the way it did all the time lately, like soda water being shaken up. "We sure don't need no more trouble."

He waited again, and finally shrugged in the silence. He wasn't the one to say what to do. Tater knew what was best. He swallowed the soda-water sting, and lay back into the cold coming up from the ground.

He didn't know how Tater could sleep with Pap on his way to town. Pap could find liquor the way ticks found warm bodies. They should at least try to stop him. Not just turn over and go back to sleep. But in spite of himself his eyes closed. He braced them open. He could hear the horses moving slowly in their hobbles, and then a train whistle, far off and sad. He wished he was back in a place with a name, in a bed without weeds in it, where he knew what to expect.

When he woke again, Tater was standing over him, poking him with his toe. He was saying, "Get up. Pap's not just snagging a drink or two off of somebody in town. He's got money."

Sammy scrambled to his knees, buttoning buttons that had come loose as he slept. "How come?" he whispered. Tater started up the hill, broken-gaited, favoring his bad leg. Sammy stumbled after him,

2

casting a glance back at the wagon. If it had been left to him, he would have told his mother where they were going.

He caught up, and they crunched through the hoary brush in a darkness that felt close to morning. At the top of the slope he tripped over what he thought was a rock. But his fingers touched smooth scrollwork. A tombstone. He tried to prop it up.

"Let it alone," Tater ordered, and swerved off into a dim road. Sammy followed closer, prickling a little to think they'd been stumbling over graves.

"Did Pap take something to sell?" he asked. "His ketch rope?"

"He'd sell one of us before he'd sell his rope," Tater said.

They could see the lights of town, pale and friendly, made by the lamps of early risers and the saloons that never closed. Cafés would be opening. People were already there, stirring up their fires and flap-jack batter.

"If Pap's got money, maybe we can take back some grub for her and the kids," Sammy said.

Tater went on. He had worked the stiffness out of his leg and his shoulders hardly dipped as he lurched along. "It'll be spent."

"Why didn't we stop him, then, before it got spent?"

Tater said, "How? Knock him down? Sit on him? I'm tired of looking after him like I was his father. For once I just wanted to lay there and not care what the hell he done."

"We could've used some breakfast," Sammy said, thinking of all the money gone. "Her and the kids." He wet his lips. "And us."

Smoke was coming from the hotel next to the depot on the outskirts of town. He could see train-

3

men in greasy caps chomping early breakfast in the dining room.

Tater strode past the lamplit windows. "I'll do that someday," he said. "Order breakfast in a place like that. Ham and eggs. Pie. Coffee. All of it. And hold out a twenty-dollar bill between two fingers, like I didn't care if it fell to the floor or what."

"Me, too," Sammy said in admiration, leaping into Tater's fantasy. "Wave it in their faces, la-di-da. I'd get ham, too. What you got." By himself, he might have chosen biscuits and sorghum, but Tater knew what was good. He hushed, sorry he had roused up thoughts of food.

"I got to," Tater said, still in his dream. "I want my turn. Something better than this."

He stopped so suddenly that Sammy bumped into him. A poster, tacked to the wall of a saloon, had the word JOBS printed across its top in dark thick letters. Tater bent and traced the smaller print with his finger. He straightened up, amazed. "Damn. He was right. This here's the same kind of notice he kept going on about."

Sammy leaned close, slowing himself a little to read it at the same speed as Tater had. It said who to go see. Pap had talked a lot about a job he'd heard of and was going to get. But they had thought it was just his trick to keep them moving on.

"They're really hiring," Tater said. He jerked his ragged cap down on his forehead where the scar had gone grayish-purple in the cold, and started off. "So, hell, let's find him and get him headed to where the work's at."

They hurried on, checking the alleys behind saloons where Pap might be warming the ground. In one, a delivery wagon had pulled to a stop at the back door of a boardinghouse.

Tater reached out and slowed Sammy. "What?" Sammy asked, thinking they had found Pap. Then he followed Tater's gaze and saw what he was seeing. A man was going inside with a hindquarter of beef on his shoulder. Sammy glanced sharply around, unable to amble on naturally and empty-faced the way Tater did. Into his mind flashed a picture of the two of them flying down the alley trailing steaks and strings of sausages.

"We could make it," Tater murmured. "While he's in there."

Instead of the rush of fear and exhilaration he used to feel when he plunged off into danger behind Tater, the soda-water bubbles sprang up again in his throat. For the first time he could remember, his feet stopped.

Tater gave him a nudge. "Hell, Sammy, decide." He moved on, wary and sure of himself, fixing his mouth to look innocent.

Sammy took a gulp of cold air. It's different, he wanted to say. This time you'd limp. Abruptly his feet started again, following.

He broke into a run at the exact moment Tater did, and felt a singing jolt of joy as Tater turned and grinned. It was the same jubilation he'd felt once, years before, when Tater showed him how to run against spring wind with his coat spread into wings. They hunched in unison, their eyes on the boarding-house door, and reached together into the off-side of the wagon.

The door of the boardinghouse opened. Tater dropped behind the back wheel with a slab of bacon, and took off. Sammy grabbed the first thing his hand touched, and whipped after him like a kite tail.

Tater glanced back. "Jesus, Sammy. *One pork chop?*"

They rounded a corner. It was a dead end. To

Sammy's surprise, Tater braked to a stop, listening, and suddenly sent the bacon skidding under a porch step. He grabbed Sammy's hand and forced the pork chop down into his pocket. Confused, Sammy whirled to double back. He swerved around the corner, full speed, and crashed headfirst into a large black lapel with a nickel-plated star pinned to it.

Two

"I TAKE IT YOU'RE BROTHERS," the sheriff said, when he had pushed them into his office.

Sammy glanced up to see how Tater meant to react. He folded his arms on his chest the way Tater did, and copied the contemptuous bend of his mouth. He hoped the color hadn't dropped out of his own face and left his freckles glaring like Tater's. He wasn't used to seeing Tater look scared. There was something more serious about this time than any other he could remember. Dread began to weigh him down.

The sheriff poked mesquite wood into a fat black stove. He set his coffeepot on to heat, and sighed. The day had started too early for him, too, Sammy guessed, gazing around in the lamplight. A gritty wind was rising, making the dim reflections in the office window shiver. He supposed one of the windows reflected him, scruffy and on guard, peeping like a turtle out of a coat too big for him.

The silence grew. He noticed that, two months into the new year, the old 1910 calendar still hung open at December. A real up-and-coming town.

The sheriff said, "Well, you favor each other." Before he could help it, Sammy followed the sheriff's eyes to the scar cutting across Tater's forehead. He was proud they looked alike, except for that. It had healed puckered, leaving Tater's eyebrow lifted as if he were asking a question. He wasn't. He already knew the answers. Sammy wished he knew. "Too bad you also favor that ugly redheaded old man of yours—he's a real eyesore."

For the first time since he had hauled them down the street by the collars, their eyes switched around to stare directly into the sheriff's face.

He said, "That got your attention, did it?"

"We been looking for him," Tater said.

"Well, you found him." The sheriff flicked his thumb at a closed door. "But I found him first, and we're going to leave him back there sleeping off his toot while we talk about you."

Tater swallowed silently and made his pale face cocky. "Since when's it against the law to walk through alleys?"

"The minute you take it into your hands to lighten a wagonload of meat." The sheriff lifted his pen. "Now, boys, I want your names."

They exchanged quick glances. Sammy saw Tater let out his breath in relief. For some reason, the fear faded from Tater's eyes. His sharp chin slowly jutted in defiance, and his mouth locked shut.

"Now," the sheriff warned.

Sammy eased his hand down over the pork chop in his pocket. You didn't see us, he said in his mind. We was empty-handed when we rounded that corner. Like Tater, he stared boldly into the sheriff's eyes.

A gust of cold air rushed over them. The sheriff frowned. Someone had hurried off the street into the anteroom next to his office and slammed the door. A girl came into view, hesitated, and walked to his desk. She put her uncertain fingertips on it. "I have to see you," she said. She had on a black coat that looked borrowed from someone with less legs and more front than she had, and she just recently had cried her nose as red as a radish.

The sheriff looked at her hands instead of her face, and said, "You're going to have to wait until I've finished here, little lady."

"I can't," the girl said. She had a soft froggy voice, as intense as a preacher's. "I have to find somebody named Doll Unger that my sister worked for. Or whoever in this town can help me take my sister back." The sheriff's gray brows lifted. "My name's Yankee Belew," the girl said. "Please. I need help. I've traveled all night to get here."

The sheriff put the point of his pen to paper. "You're wasting your time coming to me, Miss—" He had already forgotten who she was. "Those arrangements have already been made."

"What arrangements?" Her eyes went round. "You can't make arrangements—not without me."

"Maybe you didn't hear me," the sheriff said, spacing the words far apart. "You wait. In the other room. Until I finish here." They locked gazes. The girl's stricken face turned a moment to Sammy, then to Tater, not asking for their help but simply seeing who she was sharing her humiliation with. She walked out. The sheriff waited until she shut the door, and said, "Last name?"

Tater stiffened his shoulders with all the insolence he could manage. Beside him, Sammy did the same. They were in the power of somebody who could get answers. Tater was going to open his mouth and reveal something terrible. Sammy braced himself to block it, but all Tater said was, "Haney."

"First name?"

"H. T."

"Standing for?"

"Standing for Henry Tate." He hung undecided. "Junior."

The sheriff drew an official-looking sheet of paper forward and glanced at it. "So that's your daddy's name, too, is it?" He studied Sammy. "And what did the old soak name you, little feist?"

Tater said, "His name's Sammy." His face looked harder, and not so pale, now that Pap seemed to be the culprit. But Sammy could feel him tensing. He was going to push it, the way he always did. Sammy cringed as Tater asked, "Don't you want to fill in the rest of them blanks? Ages and addresses and what we nearly had for breakfast? I'm seventeen and he's thirteen."

He made them both a year older than they were, but Sammy's face didn't change.

The sheriff said, "I have the facts I want, son. You're camped down below the cemetery, illegal, a whole litter of you. Wide-track wagon, white-legged sorrels. You don't have an address, but I can guess where you're headed. And I already know where you're from."

Tater stared, then caught himself and braced his mouth into a grin. "So?" he asked.

The sheriff looked past them at something. They turned. The girl had opened the door to the little room. She said, "You're going to have to talk to

10

me. It can't wait. It wouldn't take you half a minute to tell me where to find this Mrs. Unger."

The sheriff sighed and got up. He clamped the girl's arm, and turned to Tater, pointing to a plank bench. "Sit," he ordered. He pushed the girl back into the outer room and followed, closing the door behind him.

Tater and Sammy turned immediately to the stove and held their red, thin-wristed hands almost against it for warmth.

"What are you so scared about?" Sammy whispered. "You went white around the mouth."

"I'm not scared." Tater didn't bother to whisper. "I seen pretty quick it was Pap in trouble, not me."

"What trouble? More than just being drunk?"

"More like Old Lady Chism sicking the law on him to get her team and wagon back."

Sammy peeked over his shoulder, feeling watched by a pretty girl in spangled tights on the calendar above the sheriff's gun rack. "She couldn't do that. With us way out here."

"The hell she couldn't. She has already, I bet." They both stared at the closed door that led to the jail. The sheriff's coffee came to a boil with a soft *blup-blup*. "I could've told Pap how to get away with it. He done it stupid."

The sheriff came from the other room, looking ruffled. The girl was right behind him, saying, "But I came as fast as I could—what's money got to do with it?"

"You need it, little lady, a lot of it. If you don't have it—"

"I *don't* have it. But I still get to say about arrangements. I'm all the kin she had."

The sheriff gave her a surprised glance. "You think so?"

11

"What does that mean?" Her plain square face went stiff. She was telling the truth about hurrying, Sammy thought. Her hay-colored hair was bunched like an unraveled rope at the back of her neck, held by a twist of baling wire.

The sheriff went over to a telephone on the wall. "It means I think I better get Doll Unger over here to enlighten you on some things." Sammy sat up, hoping to see how a telephone worked, but the sheriff suddenly shoved the lighted lamp into Tater's hands. "You two boys get in there and visit your old man, if he's not too pickled to know you." Scowling, he waved them off.

Tater scowled back long enough to show he didn't take orders, and crossed broken-gaited to the door. He swung it open, and Sammy followed him down a narrow passage that smelled like vomit. At the end was a cell where someone in the shadows was taking a leak in a bucket.

Their father came slowly into the light, buttoning up, and leaned his grizzled face between two bars. He said without surprise, "Well, boys. You here to fetch me or join me?"

He squinted into the light, grinning somewhere behind his scraggly scrub-brush mustache as they gazed at him. Tater said softly, "Old Lady Chism's tracked you down, Pap. She's going to nail you."

Pap wet his lips and went on smiling.

"Somewhere along the way you had to blab about light-fingering her team, didn't you?" Tater poked his face toward his father's, dropping his voice even lower. "What in tarnation give you the idea to sell that gun and get yourself all liquored up?"

Pap untied his stringy bandanna and dipped it into a tin basin. He wiped his eyes, then his tongue, then the front of his jacket. "What gun?"

"You know what gun," Tater hissed. "It was gone from your roll this morning."

Pap glanced down the passage at the door still ajar, and slowly tasted the corners of his mouth. "I was doing you a favor, boy. It's off our backs now."

"It never ought to *been* on our backs in the first place—you ought to left it rusting where it fell and never gone looking for it. All that was over with."

"All what?" Sammy whispered, coming closer. Those words and hints belonged with the puzzle pieces he'd been collecting for the last four months. They fitted somehow with the jerks and mumbles of Tater's sweaty nightmares. They fitted with the silences that always followed his questions.

"That's how much you know," Pap said to Tater. "You think those sambos ever forget? They call in some big buck cousin and you wake up in the night with a razor laid across your throat."

Tater slowly lifted the lamp into his father's face. "Is that why you yanked us up and set off on this hell-for-nowhere trip? Before she even got her strength back? Or the baby was hardly cold?" His thin voice climbed up in disbelief. "Is *that* why—because you was seeing jigaboos behind the bushes?"

"It was to save your hide, boy."

Sammy braced himself. Answers were coming.

"Pap," Tater said wearily, "it had blowed over. A thing like that blows over. You didn't have to haul us out here in the middle of winter with no place to go to." He remembered his voice and dropped it again. "And now you've drunk up the last cent we had, and bragged around how you stole a team and wagon—"

"Shut your mouth," Pap warned. "I don't brag myself into jail. I drink myself. If she's traced us she done it without me helping." He felt along the mattress ticking until he found his hat. Peevishly he smoothed the crushed black felt with his cuff and creased the high crown. "You just remember it was *you* I was helping." He jammed the hat on his head and turned to Sammy. "What the deuce are you doing here?"

Sammy instinctively stepped behind Tater's elbow. "I don't know—we was hunting you—"

"And can't even do that without stumbling over a sheriff?" Pap asked.

Tater said, "At least he didn't stumble over *us* drunk in the street like he done you—while your kids are going without eating. What the hell happened to that fancy job you heard about? You're sure getting to it in a hurry."

"Don't you lip me, boy, just because you're on that side of the bars." Pap's hand shot out and caught Tater's coat front. "And don't you blame me for what you brought on yourself and the whole bunch of us with your craziness." He yanked Tater closer. Sammy grabbed the falling lamp. "You cursed us—even that poor little baby born dead for punishment." He jerked Tater so hard his nose smashed against a bar.

"Damn it!" Tater gasped. "I didn't kill no baby. It died. What I killed was a nigger twice my size that you didn't have the guts to look straight in the eye!"

He went abruptly silent, staring at the door of the office. His thin fingers strained to break his father's grip, and finally dropped to his sides. Sammy froze, still rigidly braced not to hear what he had just heard.

"Name of God, Pap," Tater whispered. "I done it for you. Don't you know that? For *you*—so you could stay. So you could work. Damned if you're going to call it craziness, what I done."

14

Sammy felt his hands move, like ice cracking and shifting, to hold the tilting lamp steady. Pap unexpectedly let go, and Tater lurched backward. His cap fell off. A little red trickle started from his nose.

Pap said softly, "Be damned, then. You been hellbent from the day you was born. Willful. Bound and determined to do exactly what I said not to do. I couldn't beat it out of you then and I reckon I never can." He turned on Sammy. "And you're headed for hell right on his heels—you know that, don't you? Admiring every damn thing he does. Copying him every step of the way straight down to perdition."

Sammy blanked his face into a windowpane that the words could slide off of. Shock had taken up all the room he had for feelings.

Pap's eyes suddenly filled with hangover tears. He turned on Tater. "I wish down to my toenails it had been you born dead. Instead of my little baby boy."

Tater wiped his nose on his sleeve. He started off, then turned back, wheezing like a bellows. His fingers twitched. Finally he said, "You owly-eyed old tank—don't you ever think what it's like for the rest of us, with you guzzling your life away and taking us all down the jake hole with you? You ought to thank God one of your kids won't have to live like this!" Sammy reached numbly to shush him, but he jerked away. "I do—I thank God he won't. And I won't, neither."

Shut all this off, Sammy told himself. Like a door. Lean on it, hard. His whole body felt solid, like a fist that had clinched up for protection.

Pap's shoulders humped in a silent laugh.

"I mean it," Tater declared. "I got to get out of this jake-hole life. And I will. And I'm not going to have to die young to do it."

15

Pap said, "You already got out of too much. You ain't paid for what you done, yet—there's punishment still due you, boy. You're going to have to pay."

"Not for no nigger I won't. I've got living to do. And, God, if I can't do a better job of my life than you done." He swiped blood across his cheek. "You wait. I'm going to step out of my fancy car in my fancy suit with my money jingling—"

"Tater, they'll hear you," Sammy mumbled, making a dazed gesture toward the door.

"I don't care if they hear me," Tater said louder. His eyes and skin and hair, that always seemed to be smoldering, had blazed into color. "They're going to have to hear me, sooner or later. They're going to be busy listening, then, instead of shoving me down the street by my collar."

"They're going to be busy strapping you into one of those electric chairs," Pap said.

"Hell, you're the one behind the bars. And I hope you're still rotting in there when I arrive."

At the end of the passage the sheriff bellowed, "You gumps cut out the racket." He bore down on them as the girl watched.

"You'll never arrive," Pap yelled at Tater. "You're the same pig slop I am." He crushed his hat through the bars and swung at Tater with it. "They'll burn you, boy." At his third futile swing he threw it at Tater's back. "They'll bury you in that fancy suit."

The sheriff caught Tater's shoulder. With a quick twist, Tater broke out of his grip and picked up the hat. His long fingers shaped it smooth, and placed it deliberately straight and firm on his own head. "Maybe. But before that happens, I'll arrive," he told Pap, and walked down the passage.

Sammy followed the sheriff. His feet felt asleep. All of him was asleep, drawn up cold and tight, dreaming bad dreams. As the girl stepped aside for them, her anxious glance held Sammy's an instant. He set the lamp on the sheriff's desk, and blew it out, for the office had filled with raw morning light.

The sheriff propelled him and Tater to the bench and squashed them down, glaring in warning.

"I can earn money to pay you, if you'll give me time," the girl said quickly, before she could be interrupted again. Her voice had changed and gone shaky. She had got an answer she didn't want, too, Sammy thought. "I can pay. It's not like you were burying a pauper. She's not some hobo you found by the railroad tracks."

"Little lady," the sheriff said impatiently, "there's some facts you're going to have to get used to." He moved his coffeepot off the stove lid. "Your sister also happens to be Miss Nellie Blue from Doll Unger's place over on Brine Street. And since you can't pay to have her shipped, you're going to have to settle for our arrangements. They're made, and they're going to be carried out this morning."

The girl's troubled eyes darted desperately, and stopped on Sammy. He looked away, with the feeling that what he had heard Tater reveal was showing on his face like a slap mark. When he glanced back, her gaze had moved on to Tater. He was sitting gun-barrel straight in the black hat, burning a hole into space with his stare.

She turned to the window. Beyond it, the wide windswept streets headed off between gray buildings toward the flat high-plains horizon. "Doll ought to be along pretty soon," the sheriff said, studying the tired slope of her shoulders. "We did the best we could. There's even a minister. Consider yourself lucky."

The girl drew a long breath. "I'll wait outside for her."

Sammy let out his own held breath as she left. It's all right, he told himself, holding still so the numbness wouldn't crack. It's not no different. He'd never heard Pap and Tater go at each other so fierce in his whole life, but that's all it had been. Talk. Maybe even lies. He gave Tater a quick glance. It was lies, wasn't it? And we're like we always been? "Ask him if Pap can come now," he whispered. "We got to break camp and move on."

Tater looked straight ahead.

A flash of resentment penetrated Sammy's stupor. He had to get out of there. He said out loud, "Can we take our pap and go now?"

The sheriff wiped a speckled enamel cup with his thumb and poured coffee so pungent that Sammy shivered. He took a careful slurp. "You two better plan on taking your old man's place on the rest of your trip. He's going to be here awhile."

Tater stood up. His empty stare focused. "How come?" he asked sharply. "What's he done? You don't have nothing on him."

The sheriff said, "When I was your age, horse thieves got a string party instead of free room and board."

Sammy eased behind Tater's elbow and pressed against its bony hardness. "What's that mean?" Tater asked. "Is somebody accusing him? Is he going to get tried?"

"He's going to get better than he deserves, I daresay." The sheriff slurped again. "Personally I'd give him five years just on the general principle of keeping trash off the street." He took their arms in a grip like blacksmith tongs and started them toward the door. "Now let me give you boys some advice.

Move on. Stay out of my alleys. Or better yet, stay out of my town. If I have to march *you* two pieces of trash in here again, you're going to wish you'd never been born."

"Hell, I wish that already," Tater said. He jerked free and pushed Sammy out ahead of him into the wind.

Three

THE GIRL WAS STANDING against the wall when they stepped out into the cold. Tater walked past her without a glance, but Sammy saw her turn her head away quickly because she was crying.

They stopped farther along where a jog in the buildings cut the wind. Tater mashed the black hat down harder on his lank hair. His eyes were empty again, focused on the spot where the rails of the train tracks met in the distance.

Sammy said, "He was just blowing off, wasn't he—about five years?" He was relieved that his voice sounded ordinary. I'm all right, he reminded himself. But before he could stop the words, he said, "Cripes, what would we do if he meant it? We don't even know where we're going." He made a creaky laugh for all the thunderbolt happenings he hadn't been ready for.

Tater looked through him and hunched tight in the cold. Sammy couldn't make his eyes go to Tater's face. He looked at Tater's hands scrubbing together to stay warm, the raw slender hands that could make things and fix things and had yanked him out of danger all his life. What did you do! he wanted to yell. You didn't kill nobody, did you? You couldn't have.

Down the street, two saddled horses nuzzled a shiny Model T parked in front of a café. Sammy sniffed, trying to turn his thoughts to hot biscuits. He scissored his fingers behind his back, practicing how to hold his twenty-dollar bill. Finally he said, "She's going to be wondering where we're at." They had been gone a long time, he realized. He dreaded returning empty-handed to the wagon. All the faces would be craned to see if they were bringing food.

Tater slowly nodded. "You go back," he said. "Tell her about Pap. Tell her I'm gone to look for work." He watched as the sheriff came out of his office and locked the door. The sheriff nodded to the waiting girl, and walked over to the café. "Look at that," Tater said softly. "Nobody's in there now but Pap. If that place caught on fire." The sheriff came out of the café, talking to a man who chewed a toothpick, and got into the Model T while the man cranked.

"Maybe we ought to get the wagon on over into the next county," Sammy said uneasily.

"I got to look for work." Tater's jaw tensed back and forth as if he were pumping up his courage. He looked at the girl leaning against a window ledge. "I need money, damn it. I need things."

"But if they really know we stole the wagon—"

"We didn't," Tater interrupted. "We just took what that old lady owed us. Hell, *she* don't need the thing—but let her have it and go to thunder. Some-body was going to nab Pap, sooner or later."

"You mean the sheriff could take it?" The wagon

21

was all the home they had. "Just dump our stuff out? Where would her and the kids stay?"

"On the ground," Tater said. "In the sleet. What difference would it make to him?" He watched the car start off across the tracks. Suddenly he struck off in the opposite direction.

Sammy broke into a lope to catch up. "You think he's headed out to where we're camped, right now?" Tater limped on. "Cripes! Wait up!"

"Why?" Tater said. "You're not coming with me."

Sammy's face clouded. "Yes I am. How come I can't?"

"Because I don't want you." Tater clomped along faster, grimacing as his leg bent. "You're not no help, always hanging on to me. Everything I do, you copy me. I don't want you no more. This is mine."

Sammy slowed, unable to believe what he was hearing. Following Tater was what he *did*. He felt a fearful emptiness. Even if Tater was just saying what he'd heard Pap say, it hurt like a smack in the face. Staying together was all there was.

Tater passed the saloon with the poster again. JOBS, it said in thick black letters. Tater slung his hand at it. "Hell, there was a job for him. Right there. Why didn't he try, for once?" He limped around a corner.

Sammy stopped on the sidewalk. The suddenness of being denied took all the strength out of him. He felt as if his real self had gone around the corner, too, and left its shadow.

In a burst of dread he pounded after Tater. "Wait," he yelled, catching Tater's sleeve. "What you said to Pap—" He struggled with his bewilderment. "That was just big talk. Wasn't it?"

22

Tater freed his arm impatiently. "I said a lot to Pap." He started on.

Sammy caught up again. "No. About what you done." He glanced around the empty street. "You said you killed a man."

"Me? I said I killed a nigger."

Sammy gulped. "But you didn't, really."

Tater stopped at the corner of an empty lot. "What's the matter with you? You getting all fired up over a jig? You didn't even know him."

But I did, Sammy almost said. Even his name.

Instead he said, "I thought he just moved away. Or took sick or something." He stared amazed into Tater's eyes, which were the same as they'd been four months ago—except for the scar—marveling that he couldn't see a difference. Wouldn't you see a difference, when it had been something that terrible? "I thought he just happened to be gone, from that same night you come home hurt."

Tater swiped at his runny nose. "No you didn't. You could've figured it out better than that, Sammy. You're the one always putting two and two together."

But I didn't figure it out, Sammy said inside. I didn't want to put two and two together.

Before he could help it, a man and four children walked into his mind, as clear as they had been the Sunday morning they first moved toward him with the strange burnt skin and crackly hair that had slowed him to a stop. There they had come, the one black family in all of Bethel Springs, spread across the road—and who was going to step aside and who wasn't?

He had dived into the brush before they saw him. To give himself time to think, was why he did it. He watched through the leaves as they approached, the oldest girl carrying the baby, the boy holding

23

the hand of a big quiet man in his prime who was riding a little girl on his shoulders. She had been holding to his ears, but Ben Sills had turned his head toward the brush, and smiled, as if he were somehow including Sammy in his family as they passed. Sammy had felt that gaze go right through the leaves of his hiding place, and into him.

"But when I asked you—" His voice began to wobble with perplexity. "Asked you why you was out all that night with Pap's old horse. And the gun. You said—" His eyes flew to Tater's face where a careful little smile was stretching. "You said you went coon hunting that night." The last word trailed off as it dawned on him what Tater had meant.

Tater gave him a sarcastic thump of approval. "There you go, Sammy. You always had the quick brain." He started off. "Now you get on down to the creek like I told you."

"But why'd you *do* it?" Sammy demanded, running to catch up.

Tater shrugged. "For Pap. Like I said. To clear his way."

"But you can't just kill off people in your way that you don't like."

"You can't? What do you think wars are, Sammy?"

"But he hadn't done nothing to you!"

He groped for a reason. A run-in they'd had. Anything. He knew Old Lady Chism favored Ben Sills over all her hired hands—Pap most of all—and the time they sold off some of her fencing, she'd sent Ben Sills out to their place to try to trace it. That had been the first time he'd seen a black man close up. The oldest girl came with him that day, but Sammy had seen her close up already, in school. Once she even tried to offer him part of her lunch when the big kids swiped his.

24

She was a real hellion. She'd whomped Tater with her book satchel when he tried to run her daddy off their place that day.

Maybe that was it.

But that wasn't enough. Not to kill a man. A jig, he meant.

"Hang it, you quit following me," Tater warned him.

He stopped, and traced the curlicues of a store-front with wobbly fingers. Like a dog that had been told to stay, he eased on, trailing at a distance.

Up ahead, Tater ducked into an alley. When Sammy looked in, it was empty. Maybe Tater had gone in at a back door to ask for work. The funneled wind caught at him, and he stepped back against a store window to wait.

He had to stop this. He had to slam down a lid and shut off the confusion coiling inside him. Tater must have had his reasons, good enough and big enough, and that was all he was supposed to think.

He wasn't supposed to remember the nightmares.

He checked the alley again. It was pretty clear that Tater had ditched him, but he waited a few more minutes. Then he went slowly back the way they had come.

He was all right. The racket inside him was dying. It was like putting out a fire by cutting off the air to it. If he didn't lift the lid, he was all right.

A fine touring car caught up with him as he turned the corner. A tall woman sat beside the driver, holding on to a big mushroom of a hat. They stopped in front of the sheriff's office. The woman got out. She had to be the one the sheriff had sent for, Sammy reasoned as he got closer, but he didn't expect her to lift out a little bundled-up boy hardly

25

old enough to walk, and set him down on the sidewalk in front of the girl.

The boy swayed unsteadily in his dumpy overcoat and knit cap while the girl stared at him. The woman watched, talking with quick indifferent gestures. All at once the girl flared back at her, and they argued. Then, slowly, the girl knelt, and took off the little boy's cap. He tottered, and sat down hard. As he screwed up his face to howl, she reached out and gathered him close, hugging him tight in her arms.

Sammy moved toward them, pretending to gaze through store windows, until he was near enough to hear the woman say, "You satisfied, sugar?"

The girl said, "He looks like her. Oh, Lord, he looks so much like her." She was crying again. The little boy's face wrinkled up with fear and he cried, too. The girl shushed him, trying to put his cap back on and tuck his ears under, while she cried through her stretched reassuring smiles.

The driver set two fat Gladstone bags on the sidewalk. "Do these go with the kid, Doll?"

The woman nodded. She put her hands on her hips and stood gazing down on the girl. She said, "Well, sugar, if you still have any doubts, we can find somebody to take him in. I can see it's come somewhat as a shock, as they say."

"No," the girl said. "No. No. I'll take him." She looked at the woman's sharp-toed shoes. "I'm sorry, Mrs. Unger. When you told me like that—I just couldn't believe—I guess I said—" She looked up finally. "I want him. He's Nellie's baby."

"Well, then," the woman said, smoothing her hips. She got back into the car. "His name's Charlie. He's quiet, he won't be much trouble to you." She unexpectedly gave Sammy a long inquiring look, and he realized he had practically joined the group.

He backed away and stared at hardware through a window.

The girl stood up and lifted the little boy in her arms. It was a pretty sight, from the end of Sammy's eye, with her back arching and the little kid's face going alert as he rose into the air.

"Listen," the woman said abruptly, "you might as well hop in. Dutch can take us on up to the undertaker's. You're going to need to leave from there anyway in thirty minutes or so."

The girl looked at the car. A wary primness stiffened her face. She said, "No thank you, Mrs. Unger."

Cripes, Sammy thought. Don't be so walleyed grand. He would have stood on his head to get to ride in a car.

The woman made a thin smile. "Suit yourself, sugar." She gestured, and the driver gave the crank a swing.

The girl gazed after them as the car sputtered off. Slowly she swiveled around to Sammy, dismayed. "I forgot to ask. Where to go."

"You should've rode," Sammy said.

She peered around the little boy's head at the two satchels, seeing what a pickle she'd got herself into. She couldn't carry everything.

Sammy sighed. He went sheepishly into the hardware store and got directions to the funeral parlor. When he came out she asked in a meek voice, "Could you help me get there?"

He eyed her uncertainly. He started to say, No, I got to go tell my mother something. But an idea came to him. "I'm supposed to be delivering a message. But I might . . ." If she paid him, wouldn't that be something to show Tater? She must have a dime, at least. That would be a loaf of bread. He hefted the two bags. He could manage them. "If it don't take too long." He started off the way the touring car had gone.

She caught up with him and made an apologetic gasp. "I got a nephew I didn't know I had. All of a sudden."

"Yeah?" Sammy said. He wished Tater could see him walking along with a job of his own already. He couldn't help checking side streets, longingly, for a glimpse of the black hat.

"My sister left home, you see." Her low voice went even darker. "Five years ago, when I was ten. She and my brother had a really terrible quarrel. So, until Mrs. Unger telegraphed me yesterday, I didn't know where, or what—" Her throat closed up, and she batted back more tears. "So I came on the train."

They went around a gusty corner. The girl switched the little boy to her other hip. Should've rode, Sammy thought. The kid was about the age of his littlest sister, Pearl, but maybe heavier, with a pinched pale face and watchful eyes.

"I feel like I'm living a nightmare all over again," the girl said. "A month and a half ago, on New Year's Day, my brother Mick was making a speech for the union, and the strikers were clapping, and somebody stepped up on a window ledge and shot him and stepped down again into the crowd and nobody knew who."

Sammy felt sweat pop out under his arms. "Was you there?"

She shook her head. "They told me. They brought him up to his room."

"Cripes," he murmured, stunned. He stopped at the next corner and looked around, too addled to remember where they were supposed to go. It scared him that he might suddenly start telling her about

28

Tater, too soon and too much, the way she was doing.

The girl waited, sniffling and wiping her nose on the little boy's cap. "I tell myself Nellie's with Mick now, and they're close again like they used to be."

That kind of talk made him uncomfortable, but he understood. He meant to be with Tater, dead or alive. Even to hell on his heels, he guessed. But that was later. Everything later. When he could handle it. He turned another corner. Doll Unger's driver had parked in front of a narrow building.

Sammy set down the satchels and uncurled his fingers. A smell came from the building. Not the plain stench of dead animals, but a smell with cigar smoke and unnaturalness in it.

"I dread this," the girl said.

Sammy bumped one of the satchels with his toe. "I guess it's worth my time to watch these here for you."

Two loaves of bread would be even better. He didn't want to go back to camp and tell her and four little hungry-bellies the news about Pap unless he could arrive with food.

The girl looked at the funeral parlor door and smoothed the little boy's back uncertainly. He twisted away, still wary of her. "If he asks me someday, I guess I'd want to say, Yes, we went in together, wouldn't I? That first morning we knew each other." She carried him inside.

Sammy sat on the step. It made him crawly to think of someone in there, laid out. All changed. Gone. Without meaning to, he thought of Old Lady Chism's rent house, and all the other ones before it—the movings and uprootings and floors left strewn with the ragged stuff they couldn't use any longer. The pans with holes. The grease stains and bloodstains and dirt and memories. He thought of the little new wrinkled baby they had left in the grave under the brush arbor, covered with corncobs so nobody would find out and blab to whoever they should have told.

He watched a wagon carrying two men with shovels cross the tracks. The door opened. He leaped up. Doll Unger and the girl came down the steps, followed by two pretty women dabbing their eyes with little wadded handkerchiefs. They smelled so good Sammy's stomach flipped. A hearse with two black horses came around Doll Unger's car, and a man in an electric runabout pulled out to get ahead of it.

Mrs. Unger said, "How about it this time, sugar? It's a long walk to the cemetery with a load like Charlie."

The girl closed her eyes, and opened them to look at Sammy, and got into the car beside the two women. The little boy began to cry and climb her shoulder.

"How about you, buster?" Mrs. Unger called over Charlie's squalls.

Sammy gave a start. "Me?" He swiped at the two bags. "I got to watch these."

Mrs. Unger heaved a bag into each of the young women's laps. "Can you ride on the running board without killing yourself?"

Sammy gulped. "Yes, ma'am." He jammed his cap hard on his head and stepped up onto the quivering metal ledge, grabbing for the windshield support and door top every which way at once, dizzy with excitement. He had no idea what to expect, but he didn't mean to get bucked off in front of everybody.

The procession turned out into the main street,

and crossed the tracks with a suddenness that made his teeth click. A man in a black suit turned his buggy in behind them. The preacher, he guessed. Then they were on the road he and Tater had hurried along in the early dark. Only this time he was riding. He tried not to grin.

They speeded up to such an undignified clip that Sammy saw the plain wooden coffin jostling in the hearse, and grabbed a gigantic breath of thankfulness for his eyes stinging, and his body tingling, and his heart banging with life.

Four

FROM THE TOP of a little ridge, he saw the cemetery and the tangled fringe of cottonwoods and willows down beyond it where camp was. Her and the kids. He went sober, remembering that he was supposed to be there, too.

The parade with its tail of dust stopped where a corner of the cemetery tilted, weedy and desolate, into a ravine. The two men with shovels had lighted their pipes and were waiting by their wagon. The girl put her hand to her mouth, looking around.

This is where we'd be put under, too, Sammy thought. Pap, the kids, her—if we died. This here's potter's field, where the paupers or strangers or criminals go. And we're all three.

The two young women got out, snagging their skirts on sagebrush, and handed him the satchels. He had to drop them to take Charlie as Mrs. Unger swung him briskly out of the girl's arms. "Keep him quiet," she said, and steered the women and the driver forward.

The preacher got out of his buggy and coughed into his handkerchief, glowering at the group with the gloom of a sick man who would rather be in bed.

Sammy set the little boy on the ground. Charlie immediately flipped to his knees and took off like a caterpillar. Sammy grabbed him back and perched uneasily on the running board of the car with Charlie clamped between his feet. The coffin already rested on two planks laid across a fresh-dug grave. It struck him for the first time that someone named Nellie, that he almost knew, was going into the ground.

He saw that all the men were bareheaded. He dragged his cap off and sat on it.

The preacher made a level place for his feet in the dirt clods by the graveside, and said, "We are brought together today by the passing of Miss—" He coughed and took a small piece of paper from his pocket. "Of Miss Nellie Blue, at the untimely age of twenty-five years. She was not—" He checked his notes again. "Not a native of our state, having been born in one of the coal camps of Colorado where her late father was employed. She is survived by a son. And a younger sister." He palmed his notes like a magician.

Charlie began to squirm. Sammy gave him a rock to bang with.

The preacher said into the cold wind, "I did not in her years here have the opportunity of knowing Miss Blue, but I would, if I could in all conscience before Almighty God, beg His mercy on her behalf today, that she might fly like a dove into His bosom, to rest in everlasting peace."

"Amen," the undertaker agreed.

The preacher looked at Charlie. "But our merciful God is also a God of righteousness and justice and

His divine laws cannot be flouted. Remorselessly the awful day comes when their full and searing weight falls upon the transgressor and smites the wrong-doer—for we are mortal, and there is no hiding place."

The girl's mouth slowly dropped. She leaned forward, her elbows jutting with surprise.

"Therefore, we who are gathered here this morning are rightfully filled with awe and trepidation," the preacher said. "For we are looking down in sorrow upon the wages of sin."

The girl took Doll Unger's sleeve. "What's he doing?" she said out loud.

"We rightly mourn a lost life today. We grieve for a lost soul. We pray for this pitiable young woman who so early in her wretched life gave herself up to the powers of darkness. Looking down, now, how fervently we wish that a hand had stayed her from her satanic descent—"

Doll Unger said, "Brother Simms, try giving us a funeral instead of a revival meeting, for Chrissake."

The preacher looked pained. "Or that some kindly counsel had caused her to look deep into the mirror of her soul and fall upon her knees in horror and remorse, before she so willfully placed herself beyond the pale."

Charlie began to whimper. "Hush, now," Sammy crooned under his breath, "before I eat your head." He was tingling. The big words, clanging out in the preacher's round metallic voice, had started reverberations of anxiety in him.

The preacher said more firmly, "Even as we grieve, let us give thanks that this poor soiled dove's tormented life can serve to remind each and every one of us of our own corrupt and imperfect hearts, and our terrible need for atonement, before the doors of death close behind us and we, too, plunge in our pride into the bottomless pit of perdition."

"What's he trying to *do?*" the girl exclaimed. "He didn't know her—he didn't even have her name right on his piece of paper!"

She wheeled and rushed past Sammy. He saw her contorted face as she streaked by, and hauled Charlie up to follow.

A long way down the slope she stopped among the gray giant-skeletons of fallen cottonwoods. Sammy waited a little way off until she turned and said, "He doesn't know all that for sure. Even being a preacher." He could see the pain in her eyes. "She's not going to hell. She wasn't bad. She loved people."

He didn't know what to say. He was already pretty used to the idea of going to hell, himself, because Pap reminded him a lot he would. But the preacher's hell sounded a lot more real than Pap's. The preacher had made him see it, gaping, and all at once he was afraid for Tater.

The girl looked up the slope. "She was so thin," she murmured. "So thin and tired." She sat beside Charlie on the ground, and rubbed his little cold hands in hers. "She must have loved you, Charlie." She looked up, as if Sammy could assure her. He glanced away. Love wasn't something he knew about.

"You taking him to live with you?" he asked. She nodded, and gave Charlie a crow feather with a streak of sky in its blackness. "Where to?"

She laid her head west. "Over east of the San Isobels."

That didn't help him any.

"They're mountains." She gazed toward the horizon as if she might see them.

"Who's there to help you take care of him?"

"Nobody." She swallowed. "Lord, it hasn't hit me yet. That I have a little boy to take care of."

"Give him to somebody."

She thought about it. "No. I want to take care of him."

The softness of her face made him blurt, before he thought, "My brother's looking for a job. He didn't want me along."

She said, "Listen, I might as well tell you. I heard a lot of what you were saying in the sheriff's office. All of you. Your father. A lot of it."

Cripes, he thought. What had they said? Everything. The gun. Everything.

"They yell a lot," he said carefully. "They say all kinds of things. Lies." He gave her an anxious glance.

"It's all right," she said. "You've had troubles, is all."

"Tater blusters a lot," he said, to protect him.

"I noticed. That's not his real name, is it?"

"Tate," he said.

"Why don't you call him that? Tate's nicer."

He was silent, because Tater had been his special made-up name. The preacher's voice rode toward them on the wind, indistinct. Slowly they started back. Halfway up he saw that the coffin had been lowered.

Suddenly he ached to ask her, Do you go to a bottomless pit, like he said, if you like maybe kill somebody?

He had broken through the rotten roof of an old storm cellar once, when he was little, but it had had a bottom. He still woke from dreams of it, sometimes, with the breath knocked out of him. That time, in the longest silence of his life, full of little scuttling snake and scorpion sounds, Tater had suddenly appeared in the sky, letting a rusty length of chain down through the ragged hole to bring him up into the world again.

But a pit where you never stopped falling, where no one ever reached down for you—that was different.

"I'm not going back up there," the girl said, angling off toward the car. The undertaker shot her a questioning look, and indicated to the others that the service was over. He motioned to the waiting gravediggers. She said, "I want to go home. I want to grieve my own way."

"You got a home?"

"No," she said. "I stay in the room Mick had. It belongs to the union. But they don't know I'm there."

"What happens when they know?"

"Out, I guess."

Over in the trees along the creek he could see a swirl of campfire smoke. She looked past him at it, realizing they might be parting. "Your name's Sammy, right?" she said. "Mine's Yankee."

He stared at her. "I know—you told the sheriff."

"Nobody's called me by my name since New Year's Day." She gave a helpless shrug as if she knew she hadn't made sense.

He hiked his shoulders, too. He wasn't going to say her name for her, just like that.

She got into the car. The others were coming. Charlie began to cry. Mrs. Unger said, "He sounds hungry, sugar."

Sammy watched the girl feel into her pocket. "I'll feed him," she said stiffly. "I can buy him dinner."

She looked apologetically at Sammy, and he could see she didn't have enough to pay him. He turned away in disappointment.

Over on the road a movement caught his eye. The

car the sheriff had ridden off in was bumping leisurely back toward town.

"I got to go," he said. He walked slowly toward
it, as a helpless boil of hate and anger began to rattle
his insides. All he could see were the sorrels stepping
along in the car's dust, pulling the empty wagon.

Five

HE RAN UNTIL his knees buckled. When he picked up
a rock, the sheriff's car was already far beyond its
reach, but Sammy threw it anyway, yelling every
obscene word in his limited collection as the car and
wagon disappeared over the ridge.

Finally he calmed himself and started down the
road the way the car had come. He dreaded to think
what he'd see when he got back to camp. He should
have been there with them when the trouble came.

Enjoy your wagon, he told Old Lady Chism.
Take it back and fill it up with your fancy goods and
clothes and food and furniture and dance around it,
you old fat miser.

His mother was standing by the flickering fire
with a bundle in her arms when he came up. The
two littlest kids held to her skirt, but Reba and Jesse
were already dragging up a dead cottonwood limb
twice their size to add to the pile of wood. Sammy
looked around at the jumble of bedrolls and crates

39

and bundles that the sheriff and his deputy had piled on the ground.

"Pap's in jail," he told her.

His mother nodded. "They said." She looked hopefully beyond him.

"Tater's looking for work." He lifted his shoulders in regret. "I didn't bring nothing."

She nodded again, and smoothed the bundle. Sammy knew it was the teapot, wrapped in a rag, that had been a wedding present from her grandma, handed down from a place—or maybe it was the name of a business, he'd never been sure—called London Dairy. He couldn't guess whether she had tried to sell it, or bribe the sheriff with it, or was just holding it safe in her arms.

Jesse and Reba lined up beside Colleen and Pearl, making a stair-step nine to two, and Jesse began to try to tell, with his voice honking and his hands wild, what had happened. Sammy watched him slobber and strain, and finally took his arm and said, "I know about it. Hush." They all looked into the windswept fire.

He didn't know what to do. He needed Tater. The shocks piled one on the other had drained him weak. He guessed he ought to make some kind of shelter for them, but the wagon sheet was gone, and the bare broken tree limbs scattered along the creek wouldn't help.

He went up the creek a way and found a little bluff that would knock off some of the wind. They carried the belongings there and stacked them to leave a spot between the piles where they could huddle against the bank. Sammy stretched Pap's bedroll over a part of it to make a narrow roof, and tied it with the lariat. He built a new fire, nearer, and sent the kids scattering to gather wood.

"I guess I'll go back to town," he said, wondering uneasily what else he could do. Food had to come next—that was all there was to it. His mother had bent to put the bundled-up teapot into a box, but stopped, and slowly held it out to him instead. "No," he said. "You keep that. Whatever happens, you keep that." She cradled it, pressing her lips tight. Maybe it was like holding the baby, he thought.

Suddenly she looked beyond him, and her face lighted up. Tater was coming through the trees. He went right past Sammy to study the shelter by the bluff, and handed his mother a sack. Its bottom was black with blood. She emptied it into a pan as the kids crept close. It was meat. A liver. Brains. Scraps of bone and fat. The kids gave a murmur of awe.

"How'd you get all that?" Sammy asked.

Tater shot him a cold glance. "It's all that was left when I found the deliveryman again. Even my bacon was gone."

Sammy shrugged as if it didn't matter that Tater had done it without him. He remembered the pork chop in his pocket, and held it out, longing to feel that burst of joy he had felt as he and Tater ran toward the delivery wagon. Tater looked at it, and turned away.

Their mother brought the iron skillet to the fire and fried out fat to start cooking the brains in. Color had come back into her face.

"I got a job," Tater said.

She looked up proud and thankful, waiting for him to tell about it. But he walked off to the pile of belongings, and stood with his back to her, blowing on his cold hands. He knelt and began to roll his other shirt and union suit and blanket into a strip of canvas.

Sammy felt his heart turn loose like a leaf and

float through sudden emptiness. He laid the pork chop in the skillet and went to stand behind Tater. "What you doing?"

"What's it look like?" Tater asked.

"Like you was going off somewhere."

Tater strapped his roll, and stood up, testing how it hung from his shoulder. He looked dogged. His jaw worked.

"You're not, though. Are you? You got a job in town."

"I got me a job too good to be true," Tater said.

"But not in this town?" Sammy heard his voice straining, as if he had run uphill too quickly.

"I'm going to be a miner," Tater said. "I'm going to dig coal."

"You don't know how," Sammy said with a numb mouth.

"I'm going to learn how. When I get there on the train. They're taking men all along the way. I signed up."

It was the poster. Sammy felt a stab of regret. JOBS. Those glaring black letters had finagled Tater away.

"Train?" he mumbled. "You don't have no ticket."

"It's free. They pay our way for us." Tater moved off along the creek and stared back at his mother and the kids hunched at the fire. "At first they wasn't going to take me. They said they didn't want nobody with a limp. I don't know what came over me, except I wanted that job so bad. So I said—" He wet his lip and followed the smoke with his eyes.

He won't have me to tell things to, Sammy thought, and an ache like the flu settled on him.

"So I said, a nigger give me this limp. And he's dead." He spread his hands. "They looked at each other, and then they signed me."

Sammy squeezed himself up, going cold. "I wish you hadn't said that."

"Hell, it worked." Tater laughed. "All at once I had a job. Easy as old Tilly!"

Sammy braced himself. "What was it like?" He couldn't look at Tater's scarred eyebrow asking its constant question. "That night. What was it like? Doing it."

Tater stared at him. Finally he said evenly, "It wasn't much. Old Lady Chism sent him out to her Hawk Hill place to mend fence, and he was by his campfire, drinking his coffee. I rode up and aimed. It's not no different from a rabbit. You're not close enough to feel different."

Shivers skittered up and down Sammy's back like squirrels. "Wasn't you sorry? Or wished you could undo it?"

You had to be sorry, he thought. That's what the nightmares were.

Tater said, "Nix on that, Sammy. You can't undo it. Is that all you can think about?"

"Pretty near all."

"Well, don't. I don't."

"I wish you *did*. You ought to. You ought to be scared the law's going to come for you. Why didn't it, ever?"

Tater lifted his shoulders. "Because when it's a dinge they mostly just let it slide, I guess. But maybe—" He rubbed his cold hands together, looking at the little group at the fire. "It was his girl that come and found him. So maybe she never told on me."

"Why?" Sammy asked. He remembered her from school, about his age but ahead of him a grade. They had watched each other.

"Hell, I don't know, Sammy. I can't let it bother

me no more. I got to get on with my life. I can't wonder why about things."

I can't wonder either, Sammy warned himself. You had your reason, and it's good enough. He said, "I saw the wagon going into town."

"Me, too." Tater shifted his roll to the other shoulder. "And I saw you up there with that bunch at the cemetery. What kind of boob idea was that? Did you just have to go take a look at a dead whore?"

Sammy felt his mouth open unguarded, in surprise. "I didn't look at nobody."

"So, what's the live one like? The one that was locking horns with the sheriff. Yankee Doodle."

Sammy said uncomfortably, "I carried her satchels for her. That's all." At the campfire his mother was handing out chunks of meat. His stomach rumbled. "You just going to leave? Just walk off? What about us?"

"What about *me*? Hell, you can grub for what you need as good as I can. This way at least I can send money."

"I'm not staying out here under no dead tree," Sammy said.

"Then find somebody's shed. A cellar." A laugh jerked out of Tater. "Go move in on the sheriff, the whole bunch of you."

He strode to the fire. His mother held out a little clump of brains on a two-tined fork. He told her, chewing, "I got to get on the train this afternoon. After I work a month I get paid three dollars a day. Not a week. *A day*."

She asked in her crushed-down voice, "Is it far?"

"Over in Colorado. Close to a town called Pegler."

"That's far," Sammy said. "You don't want that kind of a job. You go way down in the ground."

Bottomless pit, his mind said before he could stop it. He snatched a lump of brains from the skillet.

His mother put her fingers on the scar slanting across Tater's forehead. She looked at his face, back and forth, making soft grating sounds that were worse than hearing her cry. Sammy saw Tater's eyes waver as he held his face resolute.

When her fingers moved past his strained mouth, he said, "It's the job Pap was going on about. It's the place he was headed for."

She took Pap's hat off his head and tucked a little row of dry grass inside the sweatband. He put it on again. It fit better. "He wouldn't never have made it," she said softly. "But you can. So go do it."

"I'm going with you," Sammy announced.

"No you're not," Tater said. He gazed down at the four little greasy faces. He took a piece of meat from Reba's hand and ate it.

"I'm going!" Sammy said. He watched unbelieving as Tater settled his roll and started off through the brush tangles. It couldn't be happening. Wildly he grabbed meat and gulped it down, preparing to leave.

His mother caught his sleeve. "They won't take you, Sammy. They want men."

"I'm a man, damn it!" he exclaimed. "I can get a job and send money back as good as he can."

"What would I do, then?" his mother said. "By myself."

He swallowed and was silent. He didn't know what she'd do, without Pap to boss her. They watched Tater start up the slope. Once a lady had given Reba a doll, and Jesse had wanted it and they had pulled it apart. Sammy felt hands pulling him. His longing slowly poured out like sawdust.

He guessed she needed somebody. To help out.

And to tell her what to do and think now that Pap couldn't. "But Tater—" he said. It wasn't a matter of need. Tater was leaving without him, and people died if they were pulled apart.

His mother went slowly to the pile of belongings and lifted a little roll. He could see the ends of his other overalls and shirt sticking out of his blanket.

"I'm sorry," he blurted. "I'm sorry." His heart began to pound. "I'll be back. With money so it won't be this way no more. I'll be back." He squatted so he could stare directly into Reba's smeared face. "You help her," he commanded. "You watch the kids. Keep Jesse from straying off or getting in the fire."

"I already do," she reminded him. "And you're not my boss."

He was glad she was a smart aleck already at seven. She needed to be.

His mother put the bundle into his hands. "Catch up," she said. "Stay with him, close. He's in danger."

He hunted in her eyes for what she meant. "I don't think the sheriff knows," he said. "He didn't act like it."

"Worse danger than that," she said, so intently that he suddenly wondered if she was seeing perils he'd never dreamed of—flames for lost souls, or God with the same iron face as her father's, in the tintype he had seen.

He wished she would touch his forehead the way she had touched Tater's, but she gave his roll a little push to show he was free to go. He wheeled and took off at a run.

Tater was almost to the cemetery, moving with long jerks. "Beat it," he called, when Sammy was close enough.

"I'm coming with you."

"Nothing doing. Get back there where you belong."

"I'm not staying if you don't," Sammy declared. He broke into an uphill jog. The gravediggers' wagon was coming down the cemetery road. They had finished, and Miss Blue was alone up there.

Tater hitched along slower, turning to study him. "You know I'm not staying. Not when I got the chance to make a grab for every damn thing I ever been told I couldn't have."

The wagon drew closer. Sammy sprinted to reach Tater. "I need to tell you something. There was a preacher, up at the funeral—"

Tater waved the wagon down. He said, "Sammy, I don't give a hoot about your preacher's line of bull."

"But that's what scares me—don't you care what happens to you when you die?"

"Not going to die," Tater said. He turned to the men. "How about a ride into town?" They nodded. He hopped on the tailgate, and tilted his head up toward the cemetery. "Laid her for good?" he asked. The men chuckled. Sammy caught hold of the wagon. "No," Tater warned. "Quit pestering me, Sammy— I'll whale the tar out of you."

"You're not big enough!" Sammy yelled in sudden fury. "Ten of you wouldn't be enough. You stink. Worm-gut!" He swerved away sharply, because the men were laughing, and a mass the size of a potato had stuck in his throat.

He watched the wagon bump toward town.

"Hey, Sammy," Tater called. His voice already sounded small in the wind. "Say good-bye right."

He swallowed down the lump. I'm not here to say good-bye, so get that through your skull, he told Tater. I'm here to stay with you.

47

He broke into a jog, keeping even with the wagon from a distance. He didn't know what he was going to do first. Something he hadn't thought of stopped him, empty, in his tracks. Tater would get on the train with his way paid. How was he going to follow, without a ticket?

Six

THE WAGON DISAPPEARED over the ridge. Sammy followed it, hobbling a little as his heels got raw through the holes in his stockings. It wasn't the end of the world—he just had to get on the train, that was all. Hop it, the way hoboes did, and hide in a boxcar. Or crawl underneath and hang on to whatever was there to hang to between the wheels. The thought of it scared the bejabbers out of him.

He couldn't find the wagon when he got into town. He looked for Tater at the depot first, and then in front of the saloon where the poster had hung. He didn't know where else.

When he trudged back to the depot, more people had gathered, but there was no black hat. He eased along the roadbed, trying to grasp the layout of the tracks and yard. Where did you hop a train in broad daylight? When someone tapped on the window of the café he was passing, he flinched, afraid he was about to be caught for what he was thinking.

He saw the girl's face through the glass, making a hopeful little smile. She came out with Charlie. They had eaten, except for the gravy Charlie had stashed under his chin. The girl said, "I don't suppose you're here to see us off."

"You leaving?" he asked, surprised. That was why she didn't have the satchels, then. They were already with the baggage. "So's my brother. I got to find him." He wished she hadn't noticed him. He had things to do.

"I thought he was hunting a job."

"He found one. Only it's in Colorado."

"Doing what?"

"Being a miner."

Her smile faded. "Not a miner for the big coal company that had the notice tacked up by a saloon this morning?"

"From a place called Pegler?" he asked, beginning to feel uneasy.

"He doesn't want that job." She frowned. "You go find him. Tell him that job's not what he thinks."

When he didn't move she gave him a little push. He stayed planted, bewildered. "Wait a minute. How do you know?"

"Because I live there, and I know what the coal company's doing. You go tell him—"

"I don't know where he is," Sammy said, spreading his arms uncertainly. "What's the matter with this job?"

"Everything. Listen. Go tell him to get out of it. Now."

All at once he didn't like her. He didn't like being shoved along, and told something alarming he didn't know whether to believe or not, and ordered to make a decision right that minute.

The girl strode into the depot. At the ticket counter she handed Charlie to a man in a black cap and said, "Will you keep him a minute?" The man added Charlie to a pile of empty mail sacks behind him. She said, "The agent that's taking men for the coal company—is he around?"

The man searched faces, and pointed to someone. "That fellow over there might know." The girl was off before Sammy could get his feet going. She grabbed a man's arm and asked a question.

The captive man pointed east. When Sammy got to them the girl said, "We're too late. The train stops at the stockyard first, and they're going to board there."

She turned on the man. "Is there any way to get somebody off that coach?"

He laughed. "Not a chance. The agent said half his wops jumped train yesterday, and he's going to fill his quota or bust."

The girl pushed Sammy aside. "Now wait a minute," he protested, following her out onto the platform. "What's Tater got into? Just being a miner's not—"

"It's not just being a miner. He's signed up to be a strikebreaker. For the company that killed Mick."

He stared at her, distrustful, while the train whistled at a crossing on its way into town.

A Model T stopped in front of them. The deputy sheriff had a passenger. Doll Unger glumly opened her purse and held an envelope out toward the girl.

The deputy said, "The sheriff thinks your sister had some back pay coming, Miss Belew."

The girl gazed at the envelope being waggled at her. Mrs. Unger said, "Take it. She earned it. It just slipped my mind, being upset and all."

Before he knew what he was doing, Sammy took the money and stuffed it into the girl's rigid hand.

Do something, Sammy begged, making fists up inside his too-long sleeves.

The girl's stiff fingers opened the envelope. She looked at Doll Unger. "I would have given anything for this, when I got here this morning," she said with soft bitterness. "I could have taken my sister home." She folded the envelope that had come too late.

Sweat popped out on Sammy as the train whistled again. It had made its stockyard stop. Tater was on it now, looking out a window, on his way. It was too late for anything but getting on, too, grabbing at whatever his hands could clamp. Because if he missed, and the train gained speed and thundered on without him—

He bolted off the platform and around the end of the freight office. A row of boxcars stood on a siding. He tore along them, slithering on loose ballast. A water tank loomed up at the side of the track with its long arm raised to smash him. He veered off.

Someone else was running. He dodged around the end of the last boxcar, startled to see how far off the ground it was. What would he grab for, as he raced along the side of a moving one?

The quick crunch of footsteps was closer. He scrambled under a flatcar and skidded around a coal chute. At the corner of a shed he crashed headlong into the girl. They rattled down on the broken stones of the roadbed. His cap flew one way, his roll another. He was up and off in a flash, snatching them up, but her foot shot out and sent him sprawling again.

"Sammy, you're not hopping the train," she yelled. She grabbed him.

"Turn loose of me!" He twisted free and ran. "I got to go with him!"

"Sammy, I'm trying to help you. You don't know how to do this!" She pounded along behind him. "What good will you be to him with your feet sliced off?"

She snatched the back of his coat. A button gave way and dropped beside the steel track worn to a shine by the grind of flanged wheels. Sammy's toes tingled as he looked down at it, and he slowed to a stop.

"Sammy, this is crazy. Your mother needs you—"

"She sent me," he said thickly, suddenly so scared his jaws locked. "She let me."

The train pulled steaming into town. Its rumbling power shook his insides. He hurried toward it as people up ahead embraced and parted. His eyes raked the windows, hunting Tater's face.

"Oh, Jesus," he blurted. "What'll I do?"

The sheriff's Model T started past them, leaving. The girl mashed the envelope into Sammy's hand and stepped out into the street. The deputy swerved and stopped as she grabbed the car door. She said, "Mrs. Unger, my sister had clothes and things—a ring, maybe—that we haven't mentioned."

Mrs. Unger glanced at the deputy. "Sure, there were a few things, sugar, that the girls divided—"

"I'd like a favor in exchange," the girl said firmly. "There's a woman and her children down by the creek. They need a place to stay."

Sammy's mouth dropped.

"As a special favor," the girl said.

Doll Unger glanced at the deputy again. Abruptly she shrugged, bested, and gave a little laughing jerk of agreement.

The girl wheeled around to Sammy. "Don't stand there looking stupid. Get a ticket. The train won't wait for us."

Sammy jumped, wonderstruck, and tore off on wooden feet, clutching her money.

"Oh, Lord," she shouted after him, "get Charlie, too!"

Seven

FOR AN INSTANT, through the grimy window of the day coach, Sammy saw the blank bleached wall of the jail. Then the train stretched itself like a row of kids playing crack-the-whip, and the town dropped away.

The girl slumped beside him, looking as dazed as he was. She patted Charlie, squirming in her lap.

Sammy glanced back once. He was sorry about Pap. Sorry to leave her and the kids dependent on Doll Unger for their keep. But he was on the train Tater was on. They were together.

The steady clack of the wheels melted his tightness. There was something he had to know. "What's strikebreakers?" he asked the girl.

"New men the coal company brings in. Scabs. To keep the mines going when the union men strike." She gave him a sideways glance. "Are you worried about your brother?"

Sammy smoothed his brow. "Why should I be? He can take care of hisself."

"Being a scab's a dangerous way to make a living," she said carefully. She jounced Charlie as he began to whimper. "What's wrong with him?"

"He needs a clean diaper."

"Those are what's in the satchels, right?" She made a wry face, embarrassed. "Back in the baggage car."

He lifted his eyes to the ceiling in disbelief. It was going to be a long, smelly trip.

"So how come it's dangerous? Do the miners try to scare the scabs off?" He said the word deliberately, tasting it. Tater was a scab.

"Wouldn't you? If they came pushing in, willing to work for the low pay and bad conditions?" Charlie let out a long, high whine. "But the scabs say, look, you quit doing what you were hired to do, so let us—we got kids to feed. And suddenly it's like a war."

A chill went down his back. A war. People got killed in wars. Her brother had.

The girl jiggled Charlie slower and slower and finally drew him close into the warmth of her arms. He shuddered himself quiet and put his hand inside her coat. She flushed and let him move his fingers over the comforting softness.

Two tears slid down her cheeks. Sammy looked away, embarrassed but in some mysterious way comforted, too, for all the bruising the day had given him.

He closed his eyes and watched the wagon pull out of the yard of Old Lady Chism's rent house in the dark. Pap and Tater sat on the wagon seat. His mother sat in the back, surrounded by children yanked up like turnips and crying, as the girl was, for what couldn't be helped.

He thought he had only rested his eyes a moment,

but when he opened them the day had faded into winter twilight.

Charlie was asleep on the seat facing them, with Sammy's cap for a pillow. The girl said, "When you get a chance, you ought to wash your hair. Really good, with soap." He cringed to think she'd been studying him while he slept. "Red hair is—miraculous," she said. "It would look nice."

He pushed up the dribbling sleeves of his underwear, expecting her to say that the rest of him could stand a good scrubbing, too, because he smelled as ripe as a skunk. But she didn't.

She said, "Is anybody else in your family redheaded?"

"Tater," he said. He wavered and didn't say Pap. He noticed that her own hair was prettier since little wisps of it had worked free around her face.

"Tate," she corrected him. "Doctor *Tate* Haney." She made it rumble, testing the sound of it. "Major *Tate* Haney. If you start calling him that, he'll have to grow to fit it."

"Governor Tater," he said, getting her meaning. He marveled at how easily they were talking. It was something new to him, and he liked it. Tater used to talk to him. But that had changed. "You got a funny name. I mean different."

"My daddy named me for a mine. Down in New Mexico Territory, before he came up to Back Town. That's the company town up above Pegler, where he worked. Until the cave-in." She fell silent. Then she said, "My mother had already died a long time before he got killed. Mick raised me. Because Nellie wasn't there."

The train slowed and eased into a little burg lit up with electric lights.

"Must be the dinner stop." She woke Charlie.

Sammy followed her out into the sweet-sharp smell of coal smoke. She took out her envelope and bought them chili at the café. Sammy mashed big crumbled crackers down through rust-colored grease while his eyes searched the crowd of passengers for the black hat, but it never came.

He couldn't finish. He pushed his way outside and hurried along the length of the train, staring inside at the dimly lit heads and shoulders. The shades of one coach were drawn. A man came from it, carrying a tray piled with dirty dishes and cups, and went into the café. Sammy ran around the train to the other side, but the shades were drawn there, too.

He tried to feel Tater inside the coach, leaning back, his pockets full of crackers he'd squirreled away. He tried to warn him: Find out about this war you're getting into.

He peed between the cars because he didn't know where to go on the train, and went back into the light of the streetlamp. He could see the girl at the end of the freight platform, letting Charlie lead her drunkenly up and down. Her free hand took something from her pocket and slowly crumpled it. She let it fall. Sammy came up beside her, pretending not to see it, because it was the envelope she'd taken the last of the money from.

"When will we get where we're going?" he asked.

"In the morning."

"What'll I do?" He looked toward the coach with the drawn shades.

"Find him," she said. "Tell him. If it's not too late."

Eight

SAMMY STARTED AWAKE in the night, pierced by the train's long wail of loneliness.

The girl, still wide-awake beside him, said, "Up at the cemetery I kept thinking about when King Edward died last year. Remember?" Sammy drew himself small. He hadn't even heard about it. "When they had his big, grand funeral in London."

He was able to nod, then. He knew about London. London Dairy.

"And nine other kings and Colonel Roosevelt were there, and the riderless horse and the crown on a pillow and everything. Did you know his little dog was there? Running along. And on his collar it said, 'My name is Caesar. I belong to the King.' "

The mystery of it struck him—the king, with all his power and doctors and money, dead, and the little dog trotting along. He wondered if Tater had ever questioned why he'd come home one night with his head split, and had healed and lived, while another man—

A jigaboo, he meant.

The train passed a little dark town. A telegraph office. One lamp. People warm under their quilts with their backs against each other. Then emptiness again.

He had closed his eyes and slumped into the corner of his seat when the girl leaned across him, looking out, and whispered, "What *is* that?"

He sat up. Out where the gray land and sky joined, he could see a speck of light. As they watched, a glow formed above it.

"A fire?" he asked. Other passengers began to stir and look.

The train moved toward it at a long angle. It grew brighter, a red unnatural moonrise in the southern sky.

"A barn, maybe?" Sammy asked. "It's big." Anxiety began to weigh him down as the red center of light dropped behind a hill, and reappeared, stronger, fiery in the night. They were close enough to see that it blazed and writhed. Smoke rose from it, lighted from below as if it had risen through a rift in the earth from some inferno.

"More like two or three buildings," the girl said in awe. "A whole farm. Maybe even a town."

Sammy wet his dry mouth. Maybe hell, his fool brain said. He tried to block off what was happening in that raging spot on the horizon, but images flared up: livestock running in turmoil, people shouting into the roar of the heat.

The terrible thing was that the train moved slowly past, unable to stop, and the blaze grew smaller, dipping behind ridges, appearing, gone again like the cries of someone being carried away. Finally it was only a glow behind the horizon, and there was no way to know if, back there in the night, people still struggled, or died, or rescued one another.

The coach grew quiet. Passengers settled back to sleep.

"My brother killed somebody," Sammy said softly. "I guess you heard that part."

"Yes," she said.

He didn't know how to go on. "I'm scared for him. All he thinks about is getting ahead. And money. Showing everybody. Not ever about none of the things the preacher was telling about." He stopped, feeling ugly and scared to be unbuttoning his private thoughts that way and letting her see. But she nodded in the dimness. "Like repenting and all that. Like going to hell. Maybe he just don't know. It's hard. I don't know. Like what's a sin or not." He wet his lips. "What is?"

She thought awhile. "A sin's when you have a feeling something's wrong to do, but you do it anyway."

Sammy gulped. That was the hard part—how did you know if it was wrong? When it was just a sambo. If a jig didn't feel as much as other people, how could you hurt him?

The girl was still thinking. "A sin's when you have a feeling something's *right* to do, but you don't do it."

She had gone too deep for him. He said, "What if you don't feel anything?"

"You can't not feel anything."

"I can," he said. "Like a hole. Nothing. Empty."

She studied him quietly before she said, "If I was trying to hero-worship somebody who killed a man, I'd be hurting."

"A sambo," he said loyally, swallowing hard.

"Oh, come on, Sammy." Her voice was sharp. "Changing the words won't help. He killed a man."

He looked out at the darkness. Without warning he had to bite down on his lip to keep from yelling, all roupy and widemouthed the way the kids did when they hurt.

"Why did it happen?" she asked.

The train clacked, matching his pulse. "Because this jig—because Ben Sills took Pap's job at the gin. And then tried to butter up Old Lady Chism so she'd fire Pap, too." He couldn't meet her eyes. "Not exactly. He got fired from the gin for drinking, but—" But what? A jig had nearly been the reason.

"So your brother thought he had to stop him?"

"He did have to. Didn't he?" He stared through the black window. "Pap had to keep his job, with six kids to feed. So one night Tater just took Pap's horse and the rifle, and rode out to where—to where—I don't know how it was." His ragged breath sounded as if it was filling a balloon. "All I know, she brought him home in a wagon."

"Who?"

"Ben Sills's girl. She went out to hunt him when he didn't come in, I guess, and found Tater, too." He could see her round black face and spiked hair. The eyes. Like her father's. "So she brought them both back in the wagon, him dead and Tater with his leg broke. And then she took her pap on, and my folks, they carried Tater in and pulled on his leg with him screaming and all of us standing there, that's the part I know about."

"Didn't he ever talk about it?"

He shook his head. "Just in his nightmares, mumbling. He yelled, sometimes. Poked me in the face throwing his arms around."

For once, words didn't come raining out of her. But he could feel her looking at him. He wished he hadn't told her anything. It was like letting her see Tater on the bed, exposed, with his belly knotted up with pain.

He looked out the window until she finally turned away, too, worming herself into a new shape against the dusty plush of the seat. Sammy felt her hand slide accidentally against his. He drew his hand away. He wondered if she was sorry she had bought his ticket. He thought of his feet left between the rails, neatly sliced at the shoe tops, as the train roared on. He guessed he hadn't thanked her.

He said shyly, "Yankee? Why'd you help me?"

She smiled with her eyes closed, hearing her name. "I couldn't figure how to get Charlie and two satchels over to Mick's room without you."

He leaned back. Do you feel me? he asked Tater. I'm right here on your train, going with you. Nothing answered. Even if you still don't want me, he thought. A troubled sadness overtook him, wrenching his insides. He let his cold fingers jerk, as if he had fallen asleep, and come to rest against her hand.

Nine

"WE'RE HERE," Yankee said.

Sammy uncurled and looked out into fierce morning light. Beyond some hills dotted with little round cedar trees like scattered buckshot was a wall of mountains made of sunlit snow.

Yankee was dusting herself stiffly. Charlie had already staggered into the aisle. A building flipped past the window. They slowed, and Sammy saw stair-stepped houses going up the slopes of a creek that shared its ravine with the railroad tracks and rows of squatty brick buildings.

He grabbed his bundle from the rack, still addled and blinking, and pushed along the aisle behind Yankee. Each window gave him glimpses of knots of men tensely watching the train hiss to a stop. At the end of the depot, three men stood under the sign that said PEGLER. One of them, with his jacket off, was buckling himself into a shoulder holster.

Sammy's heart began to thud. "Stay close," Yankee cautioned, as he jumped down from the train.

Instead, he pushed past her toward the coach with the drawn shades. Men were shuffling out of it and lining up in two rows beside the tracks. Suddenly he saw the black hat. As he started toward it, Yankee's hand spun him around. "Listen to me when I tell you something!" Her eyes were blazing.

"But I see him!" Sammy stretched toward the wavery rows of men holding their bedrolls. Tater was right there, rumpled and pale, revolving slowly to take everything in. "You said get to him fast—"

She drew him back against the station wall. "I didn't know it would be like this."

"Like what?" His heart began to thud.

Before she could answer, a group of men swinging ax handles surged around the engine and down the side of the train. "Like dangerous. Just don't move from here," she warned him. She gathered Charlie tight in her arms. "No matter what."

"Are those the miners that struck?" Sammy asked, staring after them.

"Yes. But the three under the sign—they're company guards."

He caught sight of another group of strikers edging toward the double line where Tater stood. They halted, glowering at the new men. Sammy suddenly realized that all the passengers getting off the train had disappeared.

Yankee sucked in her breath. A little man in a ragged coat had burst from one of the rows of strikebreakers, and was waving his arms. "Nem!" he shouted to the others, shaking his head frantically. "Vigyázz!"

"What's he saying?" Sammy leaped sideways as the three men from the platform rushed past him. One of them swept back his jacket and pulled a revolver from a holster in his hip pocket. Yankee gasped again, flattening Charlie against the wall. The little man down the tracks snatched at someone in line, struggling for the words he wanted. "Nem! Do not work! Do not work!" Sammy saw Tater bend out from the row, curious. Jesus, listen to him, Sammy tried to say to Tater. He knows what Yankee knows. Listen to him.

The three guards ran toward the line. For a moment the little man hesitated, then streaked off, gripping himself small.

The guard with the revolver fired. Dirt jumped up behind the running man and he hunched even tighter, zigzagging like a rail fence. But don't follow him! Sammy begged Tater. Stay in line!

The little man veered sharply toward them. Sammy saw his ashen old-country face. He felt Yankee gather herself up and step out into his path.

"Union hall!" she shouted to him, flinging her hand toward a spot in the distance. The man swerved off in that direction. As he dove through a narrow alley, a crowd of curious men flowed in behind him, blocking off the guards. They came to a jumbled stop. The one with the revolver pointed it wildly, shouting, "Move or I'll blast the lot of you!"

"What were you doing?" Sammy demanded, as Yankee sagged back against the wall.

"I thought somebody there could help him hide, or get away." The color had dropped out of her face.

The miners backtracked in confusion, and parted. The little man was gone. The frustrated guard took a punch at the nearest man he saw, and yelled to the agent at the tracks, "Move those scabs. Get them out of here."

The wavering lines of strikebreakers began to pour around the end of the caboose. Sammy hunted the black hat. He saw Tater trip on the tracks and catch himself just as he disappeared from view.

"Where's he going?" he exclaimed.

"Up to the mine, I guess." Yankee jerked her head toward a road curving off behind cedar-covered hills.

"But he don't know I'm here!"

The guard with the shoulder holster pulled his revolver, too, and the three of them hurried over to the coach, turning to face the strikers who were converging on them. From the corner of his eye Sammy glimpsed Tater and the new men jostling raggedly past an opening between two buildings. A man on horseback appeared, bending from the saddle to urge them along.

Behind him on the platform someone shouted after them, "Go work in your own country, you Bohunk scabs—we're closed down!" Sammy turned to see who was calling Tater a foreigner.

Nearer the tracks, other miners began to shout at the guards. The line of marching men appeared again, almost on the edge of town. Too far away now even to follow the one black hat that mattered. By the train he saw a big man working his way through a group of strikers, coaxing, pounding shoulders, forcing their sullen faces to turn to him.

The train whistle blew so startlingly close that Sammy jumped. The coaches shuddered and began to move. The three guards walked off very slowly like tomcats sauntering away from danger.

The big man shouted, "Nikos. Anton. Get your men home. You're giving the company exactly the excuse they want for calling in militia."

"Who's he?" Sammy wanted to know.

"His name's Ekert," Yankee said. "He was Mick's boss."

Sammy leaned against the wall, as weak as watered milk. A cloudburst had just passed over him, with lightning so close it had crinkled his hair. He had almost seen a running man shot in the back. He couldn't stop his mind from thinking, You ride up. Bam. Like with rabbits.

"Where's Tater gone?" he asked.

Yankee ventured out a few steps on the platform. "I thought they were headed right on up to start work, but they're not taking the mine road. There's a boardinghouse over in that direction. Maybe—"

"You mean he might not live up at the company town?"

"Well, there's a rooming house up there for the single men, but if the company hasn't moved the strikers out, the new men'll have to stay someplace else." She watched the strikers slowly scattering and regrouping like bees. "Maybe the company's afraid to try to get them inside the gate, without more guards."

"What gate?"

"All the mine property's behind a big fence. There's probably other union men up there, waiting to stop them."

Anxiety gathered in him again. He had liked the idea of Tater getting to stay in town. Findable. But she made any place he might be sent sound dangerous.

She said, "I guess they'll even have guards there at the boardinghouse."

"How'll I get to talk to him, then, with guards everywhere?"

She looked uncertain. "We'll find a way."

"But I need to, *now*," he insisted.

She lifted her shoulders in regret, and went into the depot to find her satchels. Sammy sighed and took them, following her glumly out into the street. The crowds of men were drifting away.

"I hope he didn't notice me," Yankee said.

"Who?"

"Mr. Ekert. When I yelled at that little man." She smiled worriedly into Sammy's puzzled face. "I'd just as soon he didn't remember that I'm the sister who might still be living in Mick's room."

Ten

THEY WALKED between buildings three stories high. Sammy's neck creaked from trying to see everything. A car came out of a side street unexpectedly, forcing them to scramble out of its way. As it jounced past them along the main ruts, Yankee stopped and stared.

"Remember him," she said in a flat voice.

"Him who?" He had seen a driver and someone in a pony-skin coat and fur cap.

"Mr. Galen Stoker," she said, as if it were a disease. They watched the car rumble up the road she had said led to the company town. "He's the superintendent."

"You mean the boss of everything?"

"Just of this mine. The company has mines all over, but the real operators live off in New York or someplace. They've never been here—to them, Back Town's not a place, it's an investment."

They went on along the narrow length of town. Behind the stores and banks and livery stables Sammy could see houses with little cow sheds and privies, and the whitewashed trunks of orchard trees. "You don't like him, do you?" he asked, sensing it.

"Should I?" she asked. "He was the man who gave the order to have Mick killed. I'm almost sure he was. But he was the man my sister Nell loved."

"Cripes," he said.

"He loved her, too. She was beautiful then, when she was nineteen. He would send for her." She pointed up the canyon the way the car had gone. "That's his house up there. He's married now. See the chimneys? Back Town's farther on. He's far enough from it not to get contaminated."

"What's wrong with Back Town?" he asked, stumped by the new word.

"Oh, Lord. Everything. The company owns it, and makes the rules, and runs it like a prison. It's ugly."

They passed a hotel. Sammy could smell coffee and see white tablecloths through a window.

"Mick used to say, Turn Pegler over like a rock, and there's Back Town underneath. I guess that was what Mr. Stoker thought was so magical about Nell, her coming out of that mean place. But then my father was killed in the cave-in. And Mick said, was she going to love a man who let greed and indifference kill other men? Mick talked like that. He said she had to decide which side she was on."

"Which did she pick?" Sammy asked.

"She couldn't pick. She left. How could she choose which side?"

Yankee dodged into the entrance of a steep covered stairway squeezed between the Odd Fellows Hall and a barbershop. Sammy followed, hauling the satchels up the clattery steps to a dark landing. She had a key on a string around her neck. It unlocked a heavy door that swung open and let them into a cold narrow room above the barbershop.

71

Sammy gazed around at the dingy walls and empty bookcases. It looked like an office. A massive desk and a grease-spattered parlor stove took up most of the space.

"I had to sell his books for my train ticket," she said regretfully, following his eyes.

"You mean you live here?" He couldn't figure where she ate or slept.

She put Charlie down and braced her aching back. "The union let Mick work here. But they didn't really pay him enough for a separate place to live, so we sort of camped here full-time." She opened a wardrobe. Instead of clothes, it had a shelf of dishes and pots. Nearly empty sacks of flour and sugar and rice lay on another shelf. She indicated a bucket. "I get water down at the barbershop." When he still stared around, she said, "Sometimes the union needed a place for someone to hide or heal up. So they had some mattresses up in the loft. We slept up there." She pointed to a ladder built against the wall. It led to a trapdoor in the ceiling.

Sammy stepped back awkwardly from the satchels. It was time for him to go. Tater was maybe stowing away flapjacks at a long boardinghouse table, eager to take first crack at the new job that was going to change his life around. Tater had a bed to come back to, tonight. He had to find one, too.

Yankee said, "You can stay, Sammy. Till you find work. Or I get thrown out. Whichever comes first." She tried to laugh.

He looked at the skimpy collection of food lying where dresses and shoes and hats should have been. "I better get on."

"Please don't," she said, and for the first time she let her face show how tired and lonely and afraid she was.

Charlie scooted across the floor and upset the coal bucket. It was empty.

She said, "I think I can find some. Sometimes the wagon spills a little outside the barbershop's coal shed."

Sammy set the bucket up again. Sometimes the barbershop's coal shed might be unlocked, he thought. He hesitated. Maybe they could use each other. Free room and board would sure beat hustling grub and a bed while he had more important things to do. He started out, to find that shed, just as someone banged on the door with a heavy fist. He snatched his hand back from the knob.

Yankee froze. "Oh, Lord. He's fast," she whispered.

She motioned Sammy up the ladder and handed Charlie up to him. He scrambled into the loft, then wondered if he should let down the trapdoor propped open at his feet. The fist pounded harder, out on the landing. Sammy sat down quickly so the ceiling boards wouldn't creak. Yankee opened the door. He heard her steady voice say, "Good morning, Mr. Ekert."

A man's rough shoes scraped the floor. The hard coaxing voice Sammy had heard at the depot said, "What the deuce are you doing here?"

"Did that little fellow get away?" she asked. "I was hoping."

She seemed to take Mr. Ekert by surprise. He cleared his throat. "He's on his way out of town, as a matter of fact. You were thinking fast, there, girlie." He cleared his throat again, remembering his reason for being there. "I forget your name. But you're Mick's sister. Are you living here? These aren't living quarters."

"I guess they'll have to do for living quarters

awhile," she said carefully. "I don't have any other place, till I find a job. I can pay you rent, then."

Mr. Ekert said, "Girlie, that could be off in the future a mile. You're going to have to be out of here tomorrow. There'll be times when we need this place for meetings. Keeping records."

Hiding people, Sammy thought. He heard the slide of drawer runners. Yankee said, "Those are Mick's. You don't have a right to look through his papers."

Mr. Ekert's voice said with chilling flatness, "I gave Mick an envelope a couple of weeks before he was shot. It was pre-payment for a job he never got around to doing. So stand aside."

Sammy hunched himself tight to keep from peeping down through the opening. More drawers opened, more papers rattled. Yankee exclaimed, "He didn't owe you anything. You owed *him* a month's pay. He was practically working free for you so every cent could go into the union fund. Get your hands off his letters!"

Mr. Ekert said, "Ah." He had found what he wanted. She must have grabbed it, Sammy thought, as he heard the sharp scuffle of their feet.

"No!" she shouted. "Not till I see what's in this envelope." There was a silence. Sammy hovered, half determined to fall out of the sky on the man. Then she said shakily, "You'll have to show me some kind of record of what you were paying Mick a hundred dollars for, Mr. Ekert, and prove he didn't do your job. My brother wouldn't take a hundred dollars for work he didn't do."

Mr. Ekert said patiently, "Don't get so riled up, little girl. There are things about this business you wouldn't want Mick's name on, or proof of."

There was another silence. She must have been

trying to decide what he meant. "Mick wouldn't do anything his conscience said was wrong."

"Oh, no doubt about Mick and his conscience. No. But all his high-minded idealism won't pay the rent, now, will it?" The door opened. "I want you out tomorrow. This is not a suitable place for you. Understand?"

He was gone. Sammy handed Charlie down and let himself down into the room. Yankee stood at the window, pale in the harsh light. She looked to see if he had heard it all, and said in a soft, troubled voice, "Mick used to talk to me about things he was asked to do. They called it pulling something off."

Sammy eased into the sunlight next to her, rubbing his cold hands.

She said, "Once they asked him to go over to one of the other mines and blow up a night-shift train that was bringing scabs back to their rooms."

Sammy shrank with more than cold. So that was the way the union scared strikebreakers off.

"He wouldn't do it," she said. "But they found somebody else who would. The bomb exploded just as the men were getting off. Bodies flying. Six people got killed. And the injured ones—hands and feet—"

"Cripes," he whispered, going prickly.

"He'd talk to me, reasoning back and forth so hard. Would maybe hurting a *few* people help the union win, and give a *lot* of people better lives?"

"Reckon what Mr. Ekert wanted him to do?"

She lifted her tired shoulders. "Kill somebody. Destroy something. Make the company think they'd better compromise." She turned on him bitterly. "Lord, why can't they work out their stupid differences without killing each other? Why can't they compromise at the beginning, instead of at the bloody end of things!"

He shrugged, too. What she was saying so passionately seemed too far away to be his concern. He needed to get to Tater, and make him leave, so none of that could happen to him.

"What do we do first?" he asked. "You going to move?"

"No," she said, lifting her chin. "Not till he comes and sets us out on the sidewalk. He might not check back for days. Weeks, even."

He felt a gust of pleasure at being included, then realized that *us* could mean her and Charlie. "What if he checks back tomorrow?"

"I better have a job." She watched Charlie pop out from under the desk like a prairie dog, alert, playing. "I think I could stay if I could pay rent. He doesn't need this place. It just galls him that I'm using it free." She smoothed her vexed face and smiled at Charlie, pretending to run toward him with little tiptoe steps. He cackled in delight.

"I can get a job, too," Sammy said resolutely. "I can help. I mean, I'd give you my pay, if—if—"

"If you can find work," she said, not seeing how uncertain he was that he was really included. She opened a satchel. "With the men out on strike, all the wives and kids are going to be scrabbling for any job there is. And businesses are closing up—that's why I lost the job I had with the bakery." She hauled Charlie up and put a clean diaper on him, tugging and folding till she got it right. She dug deep into her coat pocket and counted the change in her cupped hand.

I owe you, he thought.

She said, "Let's go see what fifty-seven cents will buy us to eat."

Eleven

YANKEE STRODE OFF down the street with Charlie scouting from her shoulder. When she turned toward the creek, Sammy said, "Hey, no. I got to go to that boardinghouse."

She stopped. "I don't think it'll do you any good. But try it. It's that shingle roof. Meet me back here."

She went on toward a little house with a cow shed. Sammy broke into a jog up the nearest street that seemed to go in the direction she had pointed. His mouth went dry. What was he going to say? I'm here? You got to be proud of me? And listen to me?

It was a big two-storied house with a sign on the porch. He crept up the steps, trying to peer into windows without seeming to. The door opened as if someone had been watching. A man glared down at him. There was a shoulder-holster bulge under his coat. Sammy gulped.

"Well, what?" the man asked.

"Are they—is this where—" He couldn't get his tongue and brain on the same track.

"They've gone on up to the mine," the man said sternly.

He didn't know if he felt worse or better. Tater had just gone off to work, that was all. Down into the dark. Men did it every day.

He opened his mouth to ask when they'd be back, but the man said, "Don't come here if you don't have straight-from-headquarters business to do with me," and shut the door hard in his face.

Sammy went down the slope he had come up. Yankee was sitting on a curb. She had bought stale bread, and had a fruit jar full of milk. She was poking soaked crusts into Charlie's baby-bird mouth. "Not there?" she asked, offering him the loaf.

He tore a piece out of it and ate with trembling fingers. "He's up at the mine." He swallowed hard. "Maybe he's fine. Maybe it's all right."

"Sure," she said. "Maybe it is." They drank from the jar in turns, as he tried to read her eyes in the bright winter sunshine.

He waited outside with Charlie while she asked at all the cafés if they needed dishwashers or any kind of help. Then she kept Charlie while he checked the livery stables and freight lines to see if they could use a boy. It was hard to come out and smile each time they were turned down. Finally they only rubbed their cold hands and asked briskly, "Where next?"

By noon they were aching with tiredness. Yankee counted her nickels and dimes and bought a can of salmon. Sammy hacked its lid open with his pocket-knife, and they squatted against a warm board fence to gulp it down. A clock boomed the hour from the corner of the *Pegler Clarion-Call*. She said, "What's so fancy about working for a newspaper?" They cleaned their fishy hands with sand. "Dare you."

He jumped up before he could think about it, and

went into the building. A man in a tight white collar looked him up and down and said, "Don't bother me if you can't read or write."

"I can," Sammy said, his hopes falling. "Pretty good."

"I can read, write, spell, or figure anything you can," Yankee said from the door. She faced the man squarely. "We're not from Back Town. Try us. Please. Try us."

"We don't hire girls from anywhere," the man said.

"Why not?"

"Because we don't." He turned away to his work.

They went outside and stood on the edge of the sidewalk. People with jobs and important things to do walked quickly past them. Down the block a wagon turned out of the lumberyard loaded with siding and shingles and kegs of nails for somebody's new house. I could build things, Sammy said in his mind. Or fix things. Or learn things. Try me. He watched the wagon pass. He had already asked at the lumberyard.

He had to have a job. Money. To prove to Tater when he saw him that there were better things to do than scabbing.

Suddenly he leaped into the street and ran alongside the big-wheeled water wagon that was passing. "Work for you, mister? I'm strong as a horse. Anything you need done."

The man shook his head and gave his burro's reins a slap to move it on. Sammy watched from the middle of the street until the wagon with its huge barrel and swinging pail turned the corner.

Yankee came out of a creamery. "They need a repairman to keep their machinery and delivery truck running."

He shook his head. He couldn't do it. "That's Tater's kind of work. He can fix things."

Charlie's eyelids were falling. Sammy took him from Yankee's arms and draped him over his shoulder. They started off again.

They tried the pickle factory on the edge of town, but it had closed down for the winter. They tried the boot and shoe store and the chili parlor and all the hotels and the store that said GROC. AND GEN. MDSE. on its curlicued sign. Charlie woke, and began to whine, fighting to get down and walk. He stunk.

"Let's go home," Yankee said.

They cut through the alley behind the Pegler Hotel. A woman was bending over a row of spittoons lined on a bench. She straightened up suddenly with her hands over her mouth, nearly bumping into Sammy.

Yankee came to a stop. "Are you sick?" she asked.

Standing straight, the woman didn't have to nod for Sammy to see what was wrong. She was so far along in the family way she looked like a pear with legs, and from the whiteness of her face he could see that cleaning cuspidors had pretty well turned her inside out.

"Sit a minute," Yankee advised, scooting a space on the bench.

"No," the woman breathed. "If they catch me sitting—"

"Sit!" Yankee ordered. She glared around. "I'll finish for you." She took the key from her neck and shoved it at Sammy. "Get Charlie on home and cleaned up, will you? I'll be along."

He and the woman exchanged glances. She sat. He went.

From the window of Mick's room, he could watch

for Yankee while Charlie played in the square of sunlight on the floor. He wondered if the woman would pay her for helping, and what she might bring for supper.

But she came in empty-handed, and washed up, and stared at the droopy little sacks of flour and sugar on the shelves of the wardrobe. "See if you can rummage up some coal along the alley," she said suddenly in a no-nonsense voice. "I've got an idea." She followed him to the door. "Don't take from anybody's shed, Sammy," she said, as if she'd read his mind. "Just the scattered stuff that would be wasted anyway. Understand? They paid for it and it's theirs."

"Sure thing," he said testily, thinking she'd have coal money, too, if she had asked the woman to divvy with her.

When he came back with a little sack of lumps, she had a pan of something waiting on the stove lid. It began to smell wonderfully of vinegar and syrup when the stove heated up. She was boiling candy.

"It's the only thing I had the makings for," she said. She poured it into a big cracked platter. "It's not for us," she said gently. "It's to sell."

She lined an old cigar box with a piece of torn sheet. Charlie suddenly took a dive that scraped the skin on the tip of his nose. Screams gushed from him. Yankee dropped to the floor and took him in her arms. "Oh, Charlie, bless your heart. Living isn't as easy as it looks, is it?" She kissed him and felt for any safety pins jarred open by his fall. "Lord, I've got so much to learn," she murmured. "That poor woman, with three already. What's she going to do?" She slid Charlie's cap off and parted his hair. Lice, Sammy thought, but she simply lifted it off his forehead and gazed at his teary face. Seeing her sister, maybe. "You know what I dream of doing, Sammy?"

He didn't, and waited, wishing she'd invite him to lick the pan.

"I dream I've got the really biggest bosses from the coal company in the same room with the union men that represent the miners, and I lock the door. No food. No water. No sleep. Until they come to an agreement and stop this craziness."

He picked a little dry dribble from the side of the pan.

"And I make them exchange their children. The little rich New York ones go on the ash heaps up at Back Town. And the miners' kids go in the big warm bosses' houses. Until things change."

He'd never heard anyone talk as fancifully as she did. He didn't know how to answer. It had never occurred to him that just anybody could imagine changing things to a better way.

She smiled. "Cut it up in really neat squares, will you, Sammy? And lick the pan."

He stacked the pieces carefully in the box. It smelled and felt so good he had to keep wetting his lips.

The room was warming up. She took off Charlie's coat. "Phew, he could use a bath. Now that I can heat some water and it's warm in here. You want to sell the candy?"

He felt a jolt of pride. "For how much?"

"Every blessed cent you can get. Then stop at the store and get potatoes and onions. And a cabbage, if you make enough."

Down in the street he didn't know how to begin. He went into the barbershop. "Nice fresh candy? Homemade," he ventured.

"Don't bother me, kid," the barber said, jacking someone upright in a leather chair.

He went down the street, asking anyone who would stop. Finally he was forcing people to listen, by blocking their way. He passed an ugly brick building topped with a flag and bell tower. He had never seen a school that big. It was probably full of rich candy-hungry kids he couldn't get to. He peeped longingly inside where they sat learning things.

He was dragging with tiredness when he found his feet taking him up a sloping street toward the boardinghouse again. If he could find out when the men would get back, and be waiting, he might manage to see Tater someway.

Two men stumbled out of a saloon as he passed, gusting warm beery air his way. They were shouting at each other, and one gave the other a shove that knocked him off the sidewalk. Other men rushed out after them, grabbing at the one who was spieling a string of words in a language Sammy had never heard before.

Something brown sailed past his head. They're throwing potatoes! he thought hopefully, an instant before he heard the crack of a bottle hitting a wall. A tall man emerged from a building across the street, feeding shells into the tipped barrels of a shotgun. He marched toward the tangled group. Several men reached to pull the shouting one back inside.

Sammy pushed closer, desperate for a buyer. "Candy—" he began. The man being towed backward broke from the grabbing hands and sent the candy box flying as he lunged off down the sidewalk.

Sammy froze, stunned. He knelt to snatch up the pieces just as the other angry man took off after the first, and the crowd started after them both, smashing candy at every step.

"Damn you!" he yelled, getting up out of the gutter. A dog that had been bounding along after the men stopped and snapped up the unmashed bits. "Get away!" He swung at it as it seized the last piece and ran. "*I* could've ate it, damn you!"

There was nothing left. Even the box was splinters. The man with the shotgun grinned and pocketed his shells.

Sammy scraped bumps of candy with his toe, going slowly numb. He was going to have to lie about this. Or make the money some other way, so she'd never know. Somehow he had to go back with a cabbage.

Maybe five bullyboys had jumped him. Nine, maybe. He kicked box splinters as hard as he could. No, he'd just got himself run down by a bunch of miners, or company men, or scabs, or whoever the hell had been mad at each other again in this stupid lock-horn town.

And it had happened because he was thinking about Tater instead of helping the person who was sharing her food and lodging with him. The person who had got him this close in the first place.

He wished it didn't bother him that he'd failed her. It wouldn't have bothered Tater.

He saw the woman Yankee had helped, going slowly down the other side of the street. Another woman held her arm. Due, he thought. He went perfectly still. It was too bad she'd taken sick. But she'd left her job back there, that somebody else might take.

He bolted off toward the hotel.

Twelve

YANKEE WAS WASHING diapers. Some already hung on a rope behind the stove. The front of her dress was wet, and the room smelled like a privy. She looked at Sammy's empty hands, and her welcoming smile faded. Charlie waddled to him, shining like a new penny. His hair had dried curly.

"I dropped it," he told her in a rush. "It got stepped on."

Her face went flat with disappointment. She slung soapy water off her elbows. "Sammy, if you ate it, just have the guts to say you did."

His mouth dropped. "The hell with you, Miss Perfectness," he blurted, grabbing the doorknob to leave again. But it was cold out there, and he didn't have any other place to go. He said, "I could've lied a lot easier."

Her face changed again. The way Tater's did, riffling with the emotions he was trying not to expose. Her voice sank. "I'm sorry, Sammy. I didn't have a right to say that. I'm tired. I apologize."

He had never been apologized to before. He didn't know what kind of answer it took. He squatted in silence and accepted Charlie's reaching hands. She had taken the joy out of his news, but he said, "I got us jobs."

"What!" She blundered into the line of diapers. They fell around her. "Where? What doing?"

"The lady took sick, or something. Your lady. And that left the hotel in the lurch and we got hired for a party that's getting throwed there tonight." He helped her hang the diapers again. "They want us as soon as we can get there."

"Oh, Sammy." She gazed at him so amazed and pleased that he figured he'd made it up to her. "Wow! I'll put on dry clothes. You wash, fast as you can." She was already up the ladder. "I mean take off everything and *wash*."

Her orders bent his pride a little, but he skinned out of his grimy union suit behind the hanging diapers. It was Tater's, actually, stretched so shapeless that they both could have got into it. And he didn't help it any by dragging the sleeves through the washwater as he hurried to scrub himself. She was coming down as he threw his clothes back on, half buttoned.

They bundled Charlie up and hurried through the cold windy dusk. Sammy couldn't tell if he stung from pride or soap curds.

In the hotel alley they made quick plans. He went in and she stayed with Charlie. A bossy lady in a long starched apron seized him and pointed out how she wanted tables moved from a storage room, and how to lay the tablecloths. The minute she left, he whisked Yankee and Charlie into the storeroom. They made a play-place behind a stack of boxes, with a tablecloth for Charlie to sit on, and rushed out to work.

They cranked ice cream freezers. They wrestled heavy oak tables and chairs into a room hung with red and white swags. "What's all the hearts for?" he whispered, pointing to the red decorations everywhere.

"It's Valentine's Day," she said aloud, not as out of place in their surroundings as he was. "Parties have *motifs*."

He had to take her word for it. He said, "You sure talk fancy, sometimes."

She grinned, laying out napkins like dominoes. "Mick said speaking is the most special thing humans do. He said, Learn those big words—they give you the advantage. And they're free."

A group of pretty girls came in, chattering as they were helped out of their coats by boys no older than Tater who were all done up in suits and ties and sharp-toed shoes. Sammy felt Yankee pluck his sleeve as he stared, and draw him back to the kitchen.

From the door he could see a slick-haired man opening sheet music at a piano. The bossy lady hissed, "The punch! The punch!" She sent him staggering back into the party room with a tilting bowl of something red with real ice sloshing in it. The pianist began to play ragtime. Sammy gawked, his toes coming alive, until Yankee darted out and hauled him back to his work.

You'll look like them, someday, he told Tater in his head. Better. We'll have haircuts like that. And fancy suits—

With a start he swept from his mind the last words Pap had yelled as they walked from the jail. He calmed himself and shot out his wrists to draw his wet underwear sleeves back under the cuffs of his shirt. The hotel's unnatural heat made him itchy and nervous. But he had to tough it through. The job might even turn into something permanent, and he could tell Tater, Sure, there's work all over, safer than yours.

Yankee said behind him, "There was supposed to be a waiter. She says you'll have to do it."

"Do what? No," he declared. He took the dasher out of the ice cream and carried a bowl of scrapings to Charlie in hopes it would keep his yells safely below the noise of the music and laughter.

Yankee found him again. "It's just serving the cake and pouring the punch. You can do it fine, Sammy. Fifteen cents more pay."

He groaned. He had worked all day sometimes for fifteen cents. He didn't know why he was standing there in that place, nearly strangling in the heat, to repay a debt—when he ached to go pounding up the road again in one more attempt to see Tater.

Yankee shoved a tray into his hands. A cake all curly with pink and white frosting nearly filled it. She gave him a push.

The pretty girls squealed, "Ooooh," as he centered it on the main table, knocking cardboard cupids on their noses. He saw, dismayed, that the cake wasn't cut. He found something that looked like a trowel and began to lop off pieces and dump them on little plates. Everyone left the piano player flailing away and gathered around the table.

He could feel the sleeves of his union suit creeping out past his shirt cuffs again and dragging gently across the frosting as he worked. One of the girls wrinkled her nose and said, "My word, watch what you're doing."

A boy with a grin like Tater's slipped a little flask back into his coat pocket and called, "Hey, Red, I just doctored your bucket of blood—where'd you hide the cups?"

Sammy scuttled toward the kitchen, and nearly crashed into Yankee bringing him the punch cups on a tray. Behind her the bossy woman was dishing up ice cream.

He ladled punch, poking cups out to waiting hands. He saw that his underwear sleeves, with some kind of nightmarish illogic, were creeping farther out over his knuckles. Their gray edges turned a delicate rose as they soaked up punch. Somebody giggled. Then a titter started, sweeping louder into gusts of laughter. The boy with the flask sputtered, "Had you noticed your arms are getting shorter, Red?"

Sammy felt his face go the color of the hearts twirling on their strings around him. "Jesus cripes," he whispered to the tissue-paper festoons above his head. His disappearing fingers tingled. The boys pounded each other's backs, convulsed. Behind him the bossy woman's apron suddenly crackled like frozen wash on a line as she reached for his ear.

"Out the door," she gasped, having a kind of seizure. "Out the *door*." They passed Yankee holding a tray of ice cream dishes. He held up his dribbling sleeves.

"Me, too?" Yankee asked.

"Oh, by all means, you too," the woman breathed, propelling Sammy through the kitchen.

He broke from her grip with the last of his dignity. "I got to get the baby," he said.

He marched a bit lopsidedly into the storage room, hoping his ear would grow straight, and pushed away the boxes. Ice cream had pretty well glued Charlie to the tablecloth, but Sammy peeled him free and marched outside. Yankee followed in a minute. They stood listening to the muffled plink of ragtime.

At the end of the alley they turned along the wall of the hotel. As they passed a window, Yankee touched his arm. They could see the party. Couples were eating ice cream. Off in a corner a handsome boy with a valentine was surprising a girl with a nose-bumping kiss.

Sammy glared at his hands in their union-suit mittens. "I'm sorry," he groaned. "Damn. I'm stupid." In the window's light he could see her shoulders shaking. He set Charlie down and wrung out the edges of his sleeves.

A funny sound spurted out of Yankee. She said through it, "Aren't they pretty in there? With their paper hearts?" She turned on him. With a jolt he realized she was laughing. "And you're worth any ten of them, Sammy. Even with your underwear mostly on the outside."

He walked away with Charlie. She followed, swallowing her giggles. "Reckon what I'm going to ruin next for you?" he asked bitterly.

She snickered. "I don't know. But we should be finding out soon."

She was trying to lift him out of his gloom, but he wouldn't let her. He said, "Could I get a job at the mine?"

She went quiet. "I guess you could. Boys do. As scrawny as you. But Sammy—"

"Doing what?"

"I don't know. Oiler boy. Switch boy. Maybe taking care of the animals."

"What animals?"

"The mules. Mules pull the cars."

"I know all about mules," he said, lying considerably.

"Sammy." She sounded distressed. "I wish you wouldn't even think about it."

"I got to. This sure ain't working." The ache of their endless walking and rejection made his voice raspy. "We tried every damn place in town. And everything I touch—"

"Sammy, quit belittling yourself. I promise to belittle you if you ever need taking down." She was trying to smile, but her eyes told him what she was really thinking. He'd be a scab, too, like Tater, if he went to the mine. He'd be on the enemy side.

"What's the mule job?" he insisted, braced against the tug and shove of his feelings. "Driving them to pasture?"

"They don't go to pasture. They stay down in the mine."

His feet slowed. "You mean—they don't come up? Never?"

She slowed to match him. "Maybe when they're too old or sick to work. But by then they're blind."

A shiver colder than the air went over him. "Cripes," he murmured. He saw them dim in some carved-out space, nosing for hay wisps in their endless dark.

At a cross street she hesitated. "Sammy. There's something I've got to do. Something I found out about at the hotel." She made an uncertain laugh. "But if I let you come—"

"I'd wreck it," he said grimly.

"No, it's just—something hard to do. I'll tell you, when I get home." She tucked her key into his sticky hand, and walked off fast in the dark.

He found his way back to Mick's room. Inside, he groped for a lamp and matches, but gave up. He didn't know where she meant for him to sleep, so he spread his roll by the barely warm stove, tucked

91

Charlie in with him, and lay waiting for her. He didn't like for her to be out there by herself. Once he heard what sounded like shots, but maybe it was rowdies ventilating a saloon. Not part of the war.

She woke him lighting the lamp. There was snow on her shoulders. Her face was excited. She said, "What are you doing? Bring your quilt up to the loft, there's a mattress up there for you." She was savoring something. She picked Charlie up, then realized that he'd have to be lifted to someone reaching down from the trapdoor. "You brought me luck, Sammy. I got a job."

"You did?" He felt a stab of envy.

"I'm going to help cook and clean at the boardinghouse. With all the new men coming in—"

He hadn't heard right. "Tater's boardinghouse?"

She rushed on. "That woman at the hotel—she knows the cook at the boardinghouse and told me her name. So I just ran and asked her before anyone else did. And she said she'd try me."

He stared at her. She had gone to Tater's boardinghouse without him. Got past a guard. Hadn't even told him where she was going.

"She said I could start—"

"Did you see my brother?" he cut in like a pickax.

"No, of course not, Sammy. I went to the cook's house. Let me finish—I knew you'd go crazy and want to check on Tate again if I took you along. You get to come with me. In the morning. You get to help me unload supplies."

His anger wilted. "I do?" A gush of gratitude filled the space it left. He gazed into her flushed face. "Early enough to see him before he leaves again?"

"Really early," she promised. "But, Sammy, there'll be guards—you'll have to be careful, trying to talk to Tate."

He sighed, feeling a calmness, finally. Really early. He thought of something. "You switched sides."

Her smile pinched out. She nodded. "That was the hard part. Going over to the company. I thought of Mick."

She climbed the ladder and lit a lamp in the loft. She reached down for Sammy's roll, and then for Charlie, still sleeping like a possum as he dangled.

"The idea of being on Mr. Stoker's payroll—that hurt," she went on, tucking Charlie in on one of the mattresses on the floor. "But then I thought, No, working there, and using his money to eat, and stay alive, and out-endure him—maybe that's the best way I could ever fight him."

Sammy blew out the lamp and climbed up. She had spread his roll over the quilts on the mattress. "You can't hate too good on an empty stomach," he agreed. He shucked his shoes and crawled stiff and thankful between the musty covers. He guessed he'd had the busiest two days of his life. When he put out the lamp, the darkness outside glowed with snowfall. He heard her drop down beside Charlie with a sigh.

"I guess I hate Mr. Stoker," she said wearily. She was quiet a long time. "Sure I do. For all he did to Mick. What he's doing to the miners. But then all at once I see him coming on summer nights to drive away with Nell. So lovesick." She shifted on the lumpy mattress. "I know nobody's ever just one thing. We can't be. But I wish he was. If he could be just the enemy, it would be easier."

93

Thirteen

SNOW WAS FALLING in the dark when they got to the boardinghouse. The woman Yankee would work for was already baking biscuits and boiling dried peaches for breakfast. An old man showed them the bags of flour and sugar and onions and coffee beans stacked under a tarpaulin in his wagon. A different guard from the one Sammy had seen the day before sat inside the door, watching as they climbed the slushy steps, back and forth, and staggered down lamplit stairs to dump their loads in a cluttered basement.

Each time they passed through the kitchen, where Charlie played behind a barricade of chairs, Sammy could hear men moving upstairs. He could almost feel their weight on his head. How was he going to find Tater, and what was he going to say when he did?

Yankee suddenly put a box into his hands. "It's soap," she whispered. "Distribute some in the rooms." She caught his sleeve. "But get back here as quick as you can."

Before he could think what he should do he was climbing the stairs. A man appeared at the top. Sammy gulped and kept climbing.

"Where you going, boy?" the man asked, towering like a steamroller about to flatten him.

He thrust out his box. "It's soap. She sent me." The man glowered down a moment, and let him pass.

He peeped uneasily into a gray room full of men. Some were still asleep, two to a bed. Some were up, stretching and scratching. One lit a lamp, but he could tell that his search for Tater, even in the light, was going to take time. If he was missed, and sent for—

A few men pushed past him, already dressed. He tried to peer into their shadowed faces as they carried him along. He opened another door across the hall. His heart thumped so fast he felt dizzy. He ached to yell out for Tater as loud as he could. Another group passed him, going toward the stairs with their shaving mugs and razors, laughing at jokes being called out in a string of words he had never heard.

He was whirling to scan every face when a hand took his shoulder and a voice behind him whispered sharply, "Out behind the jakes. Get!" He spun around, but a wedge of men pushed him aside on their way to the stairs, and all he saw was Tater's back.

He leaned against the wall and calmed himself. They were together. He moved obediently down the steps. His world had order again. He knew what to do.

He tore past Yankee, shoving the soap box into

her hands, and ran off across the yard. Inside the foggy windows of a washhouse, he could see rows of men shaving over tin basins. The privy beyond was so long it looked like a six-seater. Hearty human stink poured through its cracks.

He scrambled around the corner of it and felt himself gripped in Tater's arms. He started to grab tight in return, with all the intense relief he felt, but Tater stepped back. They both glanced cautiously around in the falling snow.

"Of all the tomfool things." Tater frowned down on him. "I ought to whale the spit out of you."

"I was on the same train," Sammy gasped happily.

"I ought to knowed you'd pull a stunt like that. How'd you come?"

"Yankee bought—" He stopped, not sure how he wanted to handle that part of it.

"Bought your ticket? Yankee Doodle? The live one?" Tater snorted a laugh. "How come you get all the luck when you're too little to take advantage of it? Where was you last night?"

"She's got a room. Up over the barbershop. But—"

"A room? Damn, I'd trade you. I got a bed with some kind of crazy yop saying his prayers all night. Don't even speak American."

Sammy's pride and excitement drained away. "This here's a bad job, Tater. You can't stay here, it's dangerous."

"Did you get me out here to tell me that? You're going to get me in big trouble. There's a guy in there—"

"I know, but she said to get you out, Tater. You can find a job just as good. Tell them you quit."

"Balloon juice, she's giving you a line of bull— this whole town's at a standstill. This is all the jobs there is." Tater looked around anxiously, and let his voice drop. "Look, we went down yesterday. It's not all that bad. It's warmer than up here—"

"Didn't the strikers try to stop you at the gate?"

Tater shot him a surprised glance. "They done a little shoving and yelling, but we got armed guards up there. They'll take care of us."

"But I saw what happened when you got off the train. That little foreigner—he almost got killed, right there."

"Was that her that yelled at him? Hell, I must've looked right past you." Two voices, laughing, came close, and faded on. Carefully he said, "What're you two doing here?"

"Stocking up supplies. We're almost finished." He wasn't going to say she'd gone to work there, and weaken his argument for leaving.

Tater said, "I got the idea she was into another line of business."

He said in desperation, "Tater, I'm trying to tell you something!"

"I heard the part about you staying at her place."

"She says this job's not what—"

"If jobs are so easy, do you have one?" Tater asked. His eyes were beginning to smolder. "Are you rich yet?"

"No, but—"

"You're not about to be, neither. Just how do you plan to get back there and help her and the kids get settled somewhere?"

"Yankee got a lady to take her and the kids in, while we're gone."

"Tarnation, Sammy. Is she going to put you through college, too?"

"What did you want me to do, leave them standing by the creek?"

"I wanted you to stay there and see after them like I told you!"

"Well, I'm here to see after you—you're in a lot more trouble than them." They glared at each other, huffing steam. He steadied his voice. "You're all I got. If anything was to happen to you, I wouldn't—I don't—" He spread his hands. His imagination had never dropped him into that degree of darkness.

"How come she knows so blame much?" Tater asked. He peered around the corner. Men were straggling back toward the house.

"Her brother helped the miners do their strike. And the coal company had him killed off."

Tater's gaze slid around to where the mountains should have been looming silent and heavy beyond Back Town. He blinked as snowflakes pricked his eyes.

Sammy waited, shivering with apprehension and cold. He said, "They do crazy things. Both sides. The union blowed up a train with strikebreakers in it. Tater, please. It's like a war. They want to scare the scabs from taking their jobs. It could be your bunch, any time. This house, even. Somebody with a bomb—"

"Sammy, somebody's going to catch us back here." Tater pivoted nervously in the dimness. "Look, I got to go. You're making me miss breakfast."

"Not yet," he begged, grabbing Tater's sleeve.

"Sammy, they do everything by the rules here. In thirty minutes they'll march us out. There's two or three guys that watch everybody and blab to the high-ups." He made Sammy open his fingers. "Don't come bothering me no more. The minute I get enough money you're getting back on that train."

"I'm not."

"You sure as hell are. Now you beat it."

"I'm not going to beat it! You got to listen to me—I've seen the money. A hundred dollars somebody's going to get to pull something off." He'd been close enough to think he had. "It's going to happen—"

Tater squatted in the snow, drawing Sammy down with him. The top of his hat brim was white, the underside black. His narrow face came close, taut. "How's that, again?"

"Her brother wouldn't do the job—"

"What job?"

"I don't know! Whatever trouble they wanted stirred up."

"But somebody give him a hundred dollars?"

"Some kind of boss from the union paid him, and then he come back and took it out of Mick's desk. But she says they'll find somebody else to do it." His fingers ached to catch Tater's coat again. "Please. There's other jobs, safer. You and me—"

Tater stood up. "I got a job. So it's too late to scare me with a lot of union flapdoodle." He looked around, black against the milky sky, as thin and awful as the leather whipping strap at school. "Get out of my way, Sammy. I got to go in."

"No." He reached for Tater's arms. "I don't want you dead!"

"Sammy, damn it, shut up!"

He felt himself being dragged along, opening furrows in the snow. As they rounded the corner the edge of Tater's palm suddenly hacked across his arms to break his grip. He felt Tater's hand swing up, still open, and swat him in the face.

He got up without his cap and stumbled after him, blinded by tears of pain. Tater stopped in his tracks so suddenly that he crashed into his back.

Someone stood between them and the back door.

At first all Sammy could see was a light-colored coat that seemed to be stuffed with hundred-pound sacks of flour. Then he realized the man in the coat was huge, and black, and blocking their way.

"Morning," the man said in an easy voice. Tater started around him. "Morning to you, too," the man said to Sammy, unperturbed. "I thought, being new, you might be lost back there." He reached out effortlessly and stopped Tater with an arm as big around as a stovepipe.

Tater said, "It was full. I got the runs and couldn't wait."

The man made a rich laugh. "You luckier than me. Sometimes I get *ask* to go round back."

As Tater started past him again, the man clapped his hand on Sammy's shoulder, still chuckling. Tater whirled with his fists raised. "Take your hand off of him," he warned.

Sammy almost staggered as the hand gave him a pat. "You know," the man said, "most of these gents is from the old country. They're used to going by rules. But you two from the good old USA, I could tell."

Tater took Sammy's arm and propelled him toward the back door, breathing in quick white spurts.

"My name's Bledsoe," the man said, walking beside them. "In case you boys needs help, you just come to me. I'm always around. All right?"

Sammy felt himself hustled faster across the yard. He could see Yankee at the top of the steps, peering out worriedly into the snow. The man slowly dropped behind them. Tater rushed Sammy up the steps, giving Yankee a sharp glance. "Hell, you fixed me now, Sammy," he whispered, furious. "I got a jig spying on me."

He jerked the door open and went in, shutting it in Sammy's face.

The man came leisurely up the steps. He touched his hat brim with a nod toward Yankee. His big fine teeth smiled at Sammy, and he went inside.

Yankee gazed down at Sammy. She said in a small voice, "Go find your cap. Then take Charlie home. He's screaming his head off and I'm about to get fired."

Fourteen

BACK AT MICK'S ROOM Sammy stood at the window a long time, watching the falling snow bandage the scars of town. His lip hurt where Tater had whacked him. He got some rice cooking with the last of the coal, and when it was done at mid-morning he fed Charlie. Charlie knocked his bowl across the room.

"Damn, I'm tired to death of taking care of you," Sammy yelled at him. "You're more trouble than you're worth." But he knew he was yelling at Tater.

Yankee came home. Her face was so pale he could see dark smudges under her eyes. "Are you fired?" he asked.

"Not yet." She hugged the stove, her teeth chattering. "I fainted. I never fainted before in my whole life. So I fainted, just when I wanted to be perfect. She said to stay home and not come back till tomorrow."

He handed her the rice he had saved. She gave him a wavery smile and ate it slumped over the desk, watching him as he stared out the window at emptiness again. "I'm sorry she wouldn't let me bring you your pay till I get mine next week."

He hitched his shoulders. "Tater wouldn't listen to me," he said. "I tried. He's got his mind set."

She said, "I'm sorry, Sammy."

"So what am I supposed to do?" he demanded, as if she were to blame. "Just let him take his chances?"

She lifted her tired shoulders, not able to say.

"I know people got to take chances," he said, arguing with himself. "To turn their life around. If he wants to try it, that bad, I guess I got to want it too, don't I? Because he's the one that knows. I'm just—" He didn't know what he was without Tater.

"I hoped he'd listen to you," she said faintly.

"You wasn't much help," he said, flaring up at the thought of it. "Me telling him you said it was dangerous, when there you was getting a job there. If it's not safe for him it's not safe for you." It surprised him that he hadn't thought of that.

She closed her eyes, looking queasy. "Sometimes you decide to risk. It's all you can think to do."

Something slowly dawned on him, that he hadn't seen before. "No, I think he likes that job. The danger and all. Being on the side where all the money and the guards and guns can back him up."

Yankee leaned away from the desk and threw up on the floor. "Oh, Lord." She shivered, hunting for something to hold to so she could stand up.

"Stay still," he said. He wet a rag and let her wipe her face, before he cleaned up the spatter. "Maybe that's what you needed."

"I'm sorry, Sammy. Thank you. I couldn't—"

"It's okay. I used to clean up after Pap when he come home tanked," he said, and put the rag out on the stairs.

Charlie tried to climb up in her lap, worried.

"Oh, baby," she moaned, lifting him up. "It's hard enough just being me, Charlie, without a little helpless boy in my life." She hugged him, rocking carefully.

It hadn't struck Sammy until that moment that Charlie was always going to be there. To think about and work to support, when she ought to be taking care of herself.

He said, "He's going to be trouble for you."

"Sure," she agreed, in her faint voice. "Trouble. Joy. Both. I'm lucky—I get to do this for Nell, to make up for the years we missed. I'll have someone to pass things on to. The way Mick passed things to me."

She looked so small and wan in Mick's big chair, smiling woozily as Charlie sat on her stomach, that Sammy brought down some of the quilts from the loft and spread her a place to lie by the stove.

She got under the cover gratefully, shivering. Charlie crawled into the curve she made. She smiled. "I'll teach you to read, Charlie. Think of all the things you'll learn."

She closed her eyes, getting warm and easy. It scared Sammy to think what he'd do if she got really sick.

After a while she asked dreamily, smoothing Charlie's hair, "Did you ever see a geode, Sammy?"

He shook his head. "What is it?"

"Just a gray rock, sort of round and rough. Only, when you crack it open there's a hollow space full of glittery crystals, so beautiful your eyes pop. I think inside our heads must be miraculous like that."

Sammy went to the window and stared out through the fog he made, thinking she might like to sleep. But she was smiling at him when he glanced around.

She'd passed a lot of silent days, he guessed. She needed a listener.

"Mick said I couldn't use growing up in Back Town as an excuse for letting my brains rust," she murmured. "It just meant I had to try harder. He'd say, Push. Move on. That way, every fork in the road gives you a chance to take the right direction."

Sammy watched her sift her memories like a pack of old letters. Her face was soft and tired. He thought, You loved him a lot, didn't you? He guessed it was the first time he had ever given a name to that look on a face.

She said, "Mick lost the fingers on one hand while he was working in the mine. They fired him. Lord, I remember how I cried, trying to cut up his meat for him. So bitter about it. But he wasn't. He began to work for the union. Night and day. Secret meetings out in cow pastures in the dark. All night there at that desk. He said it was worth some fingers, if he could get a law passed to protect somebody else from what happened to him."

Block it, Sammy ordered his mind. Someone had stepped up into a windowsill, and, quick as a shot, Mick and all that hopefulness was gone. "What was it like up there in Back Town?" he asked, before the sound could echo.

"I remember the whistle," she said softly. "I remember my blood turning cold because that whistle meant another coal fall or runaway car had killed a man."

"But it's better now," he said. He couldn't leave it like that in his mind, not with Tater down there in the dark.

She shrugged. "In some ways. Better than when Mick started to work for sixty cents a day, twelve-hour days, six days a week. Better than when men got loaded up in cattle cars and dumped out in the desert for trying to join the union."

He had never heard about that. In school or anywhere. He studied her, huddled in her quilt, fitting together the things that had made her who she was.

"Mick would get so mad," she said. "People from at least twenty different countries work in the mine, and it made him furious that the company helped the Irish hate the Mexicans and the Greeks hate the Italians and everybody look down on the Japanese—so they'd never get together and stand up for their rights."

"Are you going to tell Charlie what happened to Mick?" he asked uneasily. "About who done it?"

"I don't know." She looked at Charlie, spraddle-legged beside her, content. "I want him to know everything about Mick. How he believed in people. How he loved the world." She drew a long breath. "And how his murderer is still walking free, somewhere. All of it."

Sammy said, "He could use a diaper." He gave her the last one off the line, and folded the others into the satchel, needing to look busy.

She hoisted Charlie's feet in his little button-up shoes. "I'll tell you someday," she promised him. "But I don't know how you're ever going to learn all you need to know, Charlie, when all you can do is feed your face and fill your pants." She tried to smile up at Sammy, but anger suddenly flowed over her face. "I don't believe in people. I did. I want to. But some of them—all right, maybe things happened to them that they couldn't help, but they're ruined, just the same. They're lost. So warped they can't be saved. Mick wouldn't believe that. But I do. They're not worth the pain they cause!" She jabbed her thumb on a diaper pin and sank back, going small and wan again, as if the puncture had let all her grief pour out.

Sammy put on his coat and cap. He didn't know what to say after her outburst. "I got to look for work," he reminded her. He had to go back to Tater and say, Look, there's jobs all over. I got one. I already sent money back to her and the kids. You can, too. "Maybe you ought to take a nap when Charlie does."

She set Charlie on his unsteady feet, and nodded. Her chin went up. She scooted herself, hugged in her quilt, to a box behind the desk, and brought out a big neat pair of shoes. Then a gray hat. Her lingering fingers picked specks of lint from its brim. "Take these to the secondhand place while you're out, will you?" she asked in her flat ordinary voice. "If they bring enough, get milk and bread and a little bit of coal."

Her eyes followed as he took Mick's things. "Sure," he promised, thinking of what he'd like to bring back to her. Mick's books she'd sold. Oranges. A valentine. He said, "I got to go to the boarding-house with you again, in the morning. I got to keep trying."

She nodded. "I know. Don't give up on him." She hitched herself close to the stove again. He had the feeling she meant more than trying to get Tater to leave his job. "You're stronger than you think, Sammy. Fight him."

He went out, puzzled, and squinted into the snow. He stopped a paperboy to ask him how he got his job, but the boy walked off in the middle of his question.

He turned into a back street he'd never tried. An old man was on his knees in front of a seedy saloon, grubbing in the snow. "Hell sweat," he was mumbling. "Can't lose my wallet. Can't lose my money." He saw Sammy, and lifted his shaky hand. "Boy, help me. Find my dad-gum wallet." He looked up at Sammy with Pap's stubbled child-face.

Sammy sighed, and kicked through the pawed-up snow. He saw the greasy old pocketbook in the trail the old man's knees had made, and picked it up. The old man dug on. Sammy held the wallet in his cold hand, and slowly looked around. No one was passing. Windows were fogged. He wiped it clean against his grumbling stomach. A valentine, at least, he thought.

But he saw her eyes as she took his gift. Her damn eyes wanting to believe in people.

"Here," he said.

Fifteen

TOWARD MORNING, Sammy dug through endless yielding snow. There was a job at the bottom, and he meant to reach it. His lungs filled with icy crystals of dread as he burrowed, inch by inch. He was struggling for air when the distant hurried clanging of a bell shook him awake like a hand.

He saw Yankee, nearly dressed, jump in the dimness and exclaim, "What was *that?*"

His fuzzy brain strained to find her an answer. Not a church. Not a train. Fire bell. He stumbled to the tiny window in the gable end of the loft, and saw early lamps and a wagon tearing past over frozen ruts.

A soft wave of fear carried him across the loft and down the ladder to the big window behind Mick's desk. A glow came from the west, almost out of sight. He banged his head trying to see its center, the bright core. He heard her say above him, "What is it, Sammy?" As if she had given a signal, a heavy clap of sound answered her. The glow pulsed. Sammy felt the window tremble. Echoes of explosions collided in the hills.

"Oh, Jesus," he said as solemnly as a prayer. "A building blew up."

"What?" she cried, scrambling down.

He didn't know how he got past her and down the staircase. Somehow he was running in the street, floundering off snow-covered curbs, dodging people with faces magnetized by a billow of smoke above the rooftops.

Maybe it wasn't. Maybe it wasn't. But nothing else in that direction was big enough to burn like that. Or important enough. But, oh, please, maybe it wasn't the boardinghouse.

Others were running with him in the morning dark as he got nearer. A delivery wagon clattered by, carrying a shouting man. Sammy began to shout, too, at Tater, with senseless rage. "I told you! I *told* you!"

He rounded a corner. The boardinghouse was blazing. Men were running in its light, and smoke poured from its blasted windows.

Four fire horses stood in the boardinghouse drive, snorting steam. The hose was laid out. Someone blocked Sammy's way as he hurtled straight for the smoking front door. Hands held him. He pounded on the brass buttons of a chest he couldn't get past. "My brother's in there!" The man shook him off and shouted orders to the pumpers at the wagon. Sammy ran closer into the reek of smoke. "Are they out, mister?" he yelled to someone else. "Had they already left?"

"Get away," the man ordered. "Everybody back." A car came coughing through the slush. Sammy stumbled out of its way. Something popped inside the house. His eyes darted to every window and door. There was not a sign of life. They had to be out. It had to have happened after they left for the mine. It had to, because no one could be alive in there.

"Everybody move!" the man shouted again.

"But my brother—" he cried as he was swept backward into the street. The icicles on the closest building crashed, one by one, to the ground. The eeriness of heat and snow was worse than his dream. He wanted to be on the train the way they were that night so he could turn away and dwindle out of sight. He gasped a moment in the bitter air, and ran around to the back. Crowds had gathered there, too, and someone was urging them away. Suddenly Yankee was beside him, carrying Charlie in a blanket.

"Come farther away, Sammy." She was winded from her run. "There might be more explosions. No telling what's in that basement."

"But Tater—" he said.

"They were already on their way to the mine."

"Are you sure?"

"They had to be. I overslept. I would've been late to work. It was past time for them to be gone." She drew him back to the corner of a building. He scanned the nearest faces, afraid to believe. Suddenly all the heads turned to the blaze as something like a box of shotgun shells went off deep in its crackling center.

"Jesus—are you sure they're out?"

"We'd hear things. We'd see them, at windows. Come away, Sammy."

"No," he quavered. "Will they let them come down, when they see the fire up at the mine? So we'll know for sure?"

"Maybe they will," she said. "You need to go back to Mick's."

"No, I got to wait for him."

"I'll look for him, Sammy. I know what he looks like. I'll find him if they get to come down."

"No!" He began to move away from her, staring senselessly into each knot of people, hunting a face he might have seen the day before. The woman in the kitchen. The black man. To prove they were out.

Yankee caught his arm. "You need to go back, Sammy. You're barefooted."

He looked at his feet far away in the frozen slush.

"You can come back," she promised. "Get your shoes."

Slowly Sammy began to walk backward, his eyes still darting everywhere. The whole town seemed to be hurrying to the fire, on horseback, in cars and wagons, calling questions through the cinders falling like red snow into the streets. He had to believe her. He looked down, connecting with his feet again, and felt the cold with a deep ache. He started to run through the icy mud, expecting his toes to shatter.

With a last glance he lurched into the entrance beside the barbershop and hitched himself up the dark stairs. Halfway up he stopped, clutching the rail in apprehension. Something had moved above him—he felt it. Something watched him.

"Who's there?" he whispered.

Whatever it was moved down a step closer. Then his eyes adjusted to the dark and he saw the lankiness and the black hat.

"Oh, Jesus!" He threw himself against Tater. His heart went off like the shotgun shells. "Where was you! I was scared you was in there." He could feel Tater trying to untangle his arms, but he only hung on tighter. "I was looking for you. You saved your hat."

"Sure I saved my hat—"

"How'd you know to come here?"

It startled him that Tater stopped pushing him away and just for a moment held him hard in his arms.

"You invited me, remember?" Tater said. "I took you up on it. I changed over to the union side."

None of it made sense. But it didn't matter. Sammy scrubbed at his eyes, which were stinging from too much smoke, and tried to draw Tater up the stairs.

Tater hung back. "Are they putting it out? Is it big?"

"Really big. It's going up. They can't save it." The door was unlocked. "But what made you come here? You acted so mad because I wanted you to leave. I told you this was going to happen."

"Anybody up here?" Tater asked, looking around inside.

"She's at the fire. How long had you been gone?"

"Oh, maybe fifteen minutes. Twenty, before the explosion." He made a slow circle that stopped under the trapdoor.

Sammy shivered. "Thank goodness whoever done it waited till all of you was out."

To his amazement Tater grinned. "Who'd want a boardinghouse full of fried Bohunks, right?"

"Jesus, Tater. Don't joke about it." He started up the ladder to go find his shoes, feeling sick.

"I can joke about it," Tater said. "It's my joke."

Sammy stopped halfway up. "What's that mean?"

"It's my joke. I done it."

Sammy climbed slowly down. "You couldn't have." His eyes searched Tater's in wonder. "Why?"

"To see if I could." Tater's smile grew broader, cracking the taut intensity of his face. "Looks like I could—wouldn't you say I done a pretty good job?"

113

"But you wasn't there! How'd you do it? You was up at the mine."

"No, we didn't quite get there. The men saw smoke and began to yell to go back and save their stuff. So we turned around. And I just jumped off with everybody and hightailed it for here in all the jumble."

"But the fire—how—"

"I'll tell you, I'll tell you," Tater said. He examined the desk, lifting objects with shaky fingers. Sammy had never seen him look so proud of himself. "What about you running and getting your little friend back up here? Maybe she'd like to know how I done it, too." He glanced down, and his smile got even bigger. "Sammy, are you off your trolley? Where's your shoes?"

Sixteen

YANKEE PUT CHARLIE DOWN, still wrapped like a papoose, and stood just inside the door, brushing ash from her sleeves while she gave Tater a long silent appraisal. Sammy wondered if Tater realized that, by leaning against the windowsill, he was forcing her to stare into the light to see his shadowed face.

"Sammy says you decided to go out of the scabbing business in a blaze of glory," she said finally.

Tater's shoulders jerked in a cocky little laugh. "After he give me his big spiel I figured I'd either get better work or blowed to hell. So I chanced it." He shrugged.

Don't say that! Sammy almost yelled.

Yankee stared, still dazed by all that Sammy had told her, until Tater said recklessly, "I just about had a bellyful of foreigners and being spied on night and day, anyway. From what Sammy said, the union pays good for jobs nobody wants to do."

Yankee looked at Sammy. He said in a small

voice, "I told him about Mick. And things. I wanted him out of there."

Yankee turned back to Tater. "So how'd you manage to do it without getting yourself killed or caught?"

Tater looked out at the smoke with careful casualness. "I just waited till they was lining up out front, and said I had the runs again, and skedaddled around the house." He gave a start as Charlie unwound and grabbed his leg. He moved out of reach. "And I went right in the back door and dropped a couple of lighted lamps onto junk in the basement, and went back just as they started off. Easy as old Tilly."

"The woman. The woman who cooks there." Yankee's face was rigid.

Tater's eyes flickered out from under her knife-pointed gaze. "She was already out. She left."

"How did you know?" Sammy asked.

"I made sure," Tater said levelly.

Yankee said, "And then there was an explosion."

Tater lounged back with his elbows on the windowsill. "Cans of coal oil, mostly. Maybe some paint cans. There was a couple of black-powder guns on the walls upstairs, so I figured some powder was likely down there somewhere, too."

Sammy drew an admiring breath. He hadn't noticed any of those things, and he had spent more time in that basement than Tater had.

But Yankee said, "Who saw you?"

"Nobody."

"You better think carefully. Being wrong could get you killed."

Tater's eyes went wide, then blank again. "Nobody." Suddenly he bristled. "Hey, just nix on the questions, how about it? I was careful."

She said, "Listen, there were men there getting

116

paid to watch you. They'll get paid to haul you off to jail if they can find you. Why on earth didn't you stay with the rest of the men so nobody would miss you? What gave you the stupid idea to come running here?"

Tater's face flattened to a mask. "I said nobody's missed me in all the rumpus. Who was there, you or me?"

"I would have been there in another fifteen minutes," Yankee said. "Charlie would have been there, too. I had a job there. And you wouldn't have known it."

Sammy's legs went weak. How could he have forgotten? She had been thinking of that terrible possibility since the moment she saw the fire above the rooftops.

Tater turned on him. "Yesterday morning you told me you two was about to finish up your job there."

Sammy gulped. He couldn't find his voice. The awful thing that could have happened to her and Charlie would have been his fault.

Yankee pushed Tater from the window and stared out. "No, I had a job, dang you, and you burned it down." She gripped her arms in a spasm of coldness. "I'd like to kick you out in the street and yell for the company to come and get you."

"Wait a minute," Sammy protested. "He done something the union's going to like, didn't he? Something Mick was scared to do."

"Scared?" she said, blazing. "Sammy, Mick didn't want burned buildings and dead bodies."

"There won't be no dead bodies," he said defensively. He couldn't budge the picture of her making beds upstairs in that building, unwarned.

Tater walked around the room, restless, making a

117

swagger out of his limp. "Don't you have something to feed to this stove?"

Yankee stared through the window, silent. The sun was rising, like another boardinghouse blazing beyond the roofs. Sammy said, "I got a little bit yesterday. But it's to cook with."

Tater gave his shoulders a scornful hitch. "I reckon I better go see that union guy you was telling me about."

Yankee turned, astonished, but her sharp eyes pricked Sammy instead of Tater. Sammy squeezed himself small. "I told him about Mr. Ekert coming."

Tater said, "I figure he owes me a hundred dollars."

Her mouth dropped in disbelief. "Mr. Ekert didn't hire you to do this. He doesn't owe you a cent."

"But it's done," Tater said reasonably. He stopped beside her at the window, brushing her with his elbow as he shrugged. "It's burning, over there. Hell, somebody must've give me orders. It's his word against mine, don't you think?"

Sammy grinned. He had never seen Tater like that, tight as a spring with his pride, and sure of himself.

"You're in trouble," Yankee said coldly. "The company'll get you for this. And the union's not going to protect you. You're just some fool troublemaker, to them, acting without orders. They don't bother with kids itching to show the world how big they are."

Sammy saw Tater's eyes go hard. All the emotion behind them suddenly smoldered like his lighted hair. "Where's this Mr. Ekert at?"

Sammy waited, but Yankee only snatched Charlie up and roughly brushed ash from his face. Sammy said, "I guess he's either at the union hall or they can tell you where. It's two streets over, by a big bank.

But, Tater, she's right about the company being mad. It's not safe out there. Her brother—"

"I want to get paid for my work," Tater said evenly.

Sammy looked to Yankee for help, but she was folding the blanket she had thrown around Charlie as she ran toward the fire.

Unexpectedly she said, "Can you keep Charlie for me?"

"Where you going?"

"Out to look for another job."

Sammy struggled a minute, feeling pulled apart inside. He said, "I guess you better take him. I—I think it'd be safer if I found Mr. Ekert and got him to come here instead of Tater hunting for him."

"Sammy," she said, "we're supposed to be moved out. I don't want Mr. Ekert coming here."

He had forgotten that, too. His mind was all rattled. He said, "But it's safer. I got to, Yankee."

She held him with her eyes so long that when she turned away it was like being dropped. Maybe she had seen Mick in her mind, making his speech while someone moved through the crowd. "Sure," she said, like a door shutting. "We want to keep him safe, don't we?"

Tater spread his hands. "Hell, I can keep your kid, if both of you take off." He looked pleased, Sammy thought, that Mr. Ekert would come to him and not the other way around.

Stonily she hoisted Charlie to her hip. At the door she turned to Tater. "You're proud of yourself, aren't you? You lay awake all night with that grin on your face, didn't you—planning this big moment!"

"Not just all night," Tater said. "All my life."

She started out. Sammy hung between them, torn. "I'll hurry," he said.

Tater straightened the grin she had knocked crooked with her outburst. "Sure. Maybe I'll catch a quick nap." He looked up at the trapdoor. "That's it?" Mock innocence came into his face. "Unless it's private up there."

Sammy hurried down the stairs after Yankee. She stood at the curb, tight-mouthed. They had different ways to go, but without a word they moved together toward the smoke that stained the sky.

Seventeen

SAMMY GLANCED AROUND as they walked, to see if anyone followed or stared strangely. He wished he had warned Tater not to stand by the window. Not to open the door to anybody but them. He wished Yankee would say something.

They stopped half a block from the boarding-house. The roof had fallen. The blaze still ate slowly, like an animal gnawing the bones of something it had killed. The firemen were gone. The crowd had thinned, but little brooding knots of watchers still gazed into the fire's smoldering depths.

"All they had," Yankee said unexpectedly. "All they'd brought from their homeland. Keepsakes and letters. Pictures of their families. In their little suitcases."

Perplexed, he stared into the dreamily rising smoke. Were they sad? How could they be? They were foreign, most of them—they couldn't even talk American.

He felt doubt collide with his admiration for Tater

in a confused wreckage of anger and surprise. The bitter air stung his throat. He remembered the boxes they had struggled to carry into that basement. His stomach hurt. Those had been good things, meant to be used, not turned to black melted lumps. He thought what his mother could have done with all those blankets. A whole house was gone, that could have sheltered her and the kids and twenty times more.

"I hate this strike," Yankee said in her wintery voice. She turned away.

Sammy wanted to say, But you're not seeing both sides. Tater was doing it for her and the kids—so he can send her money.

He struggled to think how much daring and cocksureness it had taken to do what Tater did. To leave the guards and spies waiting in the street and go in and heave lamps down the stairs—the audacity of it sent a thrill down his back. "The union's going to be glad of this," he said, wanting her assurance. "This'll scare away scabs, the way they want."

"What did it help?" she asked, walking faster. "What did it solve? Some landlord lost his livelihood. Somebody at the company will say, Let's burn something of theirs—the union hall, the soup kitchen—and where's it going to end?"

He didn't know how to answer. He hadn't thought of all that. He'd thought of Tater and his danger. His feelings contradicted each other crazily, like those icicles sparkling in flames.

They stopped in front of the union hall, and glanced at each other. He said, "If you'll wait for me, we can take turns holding Charlie and asking at places." She looked a long time at the mountains in their new snow, and nodded. He went in. Beans were cooking in the back somewhere. A man writing in a ledger beckoned him into a small room. "Mr. Ekert," Sammy murmured. "I need Mr. Ekert."

"You'll have to leave a message, then," the man said. "He's occupied at the moment."

I bet, Sammy thought. Figuring out the fire. He hesitated. Could he trust a stranger? He needed Tater. "Can I write it?" he asked. The man shoved him a pencil and sheet of paper. "I mean like a letter." The man gave him an odd look and found an envelope. Sammy licked the pencil. He could be setting all of them out into the street with no place to go. He wondered how Yankee could let him.

Finally he wrote laboriously, *Mr. Ekert come to Micks above the barbar shop its about the bording house fire.* He sealed the letter up, still not sure he was doing the right thing. At least he was doing it the safest way he knew of. He went out and took Charlie from her arms.

They tried a crooked street lined with saloons and pawnshops and cheap hotels. At the secondhand store she asked, "Did you check about getting work here when you came yesterday?"

"He stands too close," Sammy said.

"What?"

"You know. He puts his hand on your back while you're waiting for him to give you your money. And gets his face close, all smiley."

She groaned. "That's all I need." She went in. Sammy tried to watch her, but it was dim inside. He craned until he could see her at the back of the store, keeping her distance from the little bent man talking to a customer.

Where was the food coming from, if Mr. Ekert didn't pay Tater? Where were the jobs, damn it? They had to have money.

Yankee and the man moved out of sight as the customer left.

He wondered how long Tater would have to stay holed up in Mick's room. In exchange for his little hour of glory.

Yankee stomped out past him, saw him, and said, "Let's go," in an icy voice. She wouldn't be working for Smiley, he could see. He hurried after her.

It was after noon when they gave up, cold and dejected, and went home. Tater was whittling a wooden chain out of an old chair rung from the kindling box. Wood chips covered the floor around his feet. He hitched his mouth into the cocky smile. Yankee made herself busy cleaning Charlie up and feeding him. She divided the bread that was left into three pieces.

"One thing they did have at that boardinghouse," Tater said, swallowing his portion in one bite. "Food. Dagos stabbing for stuff so fast they was forking each other's hands."

Sammy looked to see if Yankee smiled. When she didn't, he didn't. He asked, "Did anybody come by while we was gone?"

Tater shrugged and flipped his thumb toward the loft. "I was warming somebody's bed."

A knock startled them all. They froze like the lion tamers in circus posters, taut and cautious. Yankee reshaped her face and went to the door. A man stepped in and looked around. His eyes finally decided on Tater. "Ekert wants you," he said.

Tater brushed the whittlings from his knees, and grinned, and followed him out. Sammy hurried to the window and watched them get into a car and drive away.

"So," Yankee said beside him. "We'll see how it goes. At least Mr. Ekert's curious."

Sammy followed the car with his eyes, still stunned by the suddenness of it. A chill struck him. "Unless it was some kind of trick, and that was somebody from the company carrying him off."

She made a grimace. "Lord. Don't get the willies, Sammy. We've got enough to worry about."

They were too nervous, after he had gone, to really hunt for work, but they went out anyway, and had the luck to get to shovel snow for the grocery store in exchange for salt pork and three potatoes. Tater was still gone when they hurried back. They put Charlie into dry clothes and looked out the window in silence as he slept, not knowing what to say to each other. The suspense was like being under water.

The car came down the street. Tater got out and it went on, spraying mud. "He's not smiling," Sammy said. Tater came up. His face was hard. He sat down at the desk and centered the black hat as if it were a plate of food he would eat. "He didn't pay you," Sammy said.

Tater turned his hat thoughtfully, hunting the tenderest spot to start on. "He wanted to hear all about it. How I done it. If I done anything before. All those kind of things."

Cripes, Sammy thought. You told him about the other time. He tried to guess by Tater's face how much he'd said.

"Did you actually expect him to hand you a hundred dollars for something the union didn't have anything to do with?" Yankee sniffed. "They can get their dirty work done by experts."

"Oh, he liked my style," Tater said softly. "He thinks I got a future."

She looked him up and down. He was grubbier than he had been. Smut streaked his jaw. She said,

125

"Maybe looking dirty and smelling dirty and talking dirty gives you some kind of head start."

"Him just thanking you, that's not enough," Sammy protested.

"I didn't think so neither," Tater said. He stretched, looking just a little bit above Yankee's stiff face. "So we talked a little more. I got your time extended. You get to stay on here a month free."

Her eyes went as round as marbles. She stared at him, dumbfounded.

"She don't have to move?" Sammy asked. "That's great. That's great, Tater."

"And your coal bin's full," Tater said. He took out his knife and pared away a dirty, broken fingernail.

Yankee wet her lips so they would move. She looked around the room she'd been given. "Thank you," she said in a faint, formal voice.

"You're just as welcome as can be, Miss Doodle," Tater said. He started work on his wooden chain again. Five links already hung free, released from solid wood by his magic, holding one another. From the end of his eye Sammy watched Yankee struggle with the sudden burden of being in Tater's debt.

She said, "I'm sorry if I sounded—" She couldn't decide how she had sounded.

Tater caught Sammy's eye and nodded toward the coal bucket. "Hows about you getting some heat going in this igloo?"

Eighteen

WHEN HE CAME RUNNING BACK with the coal, Yankee was holding Charlie and saying stiffly, "I'll let him stay here, then. Because it'll be warmer for him."

"You leaving again?" Sammy asked.

She said, "Your brother bargained himself a place to stay from Mr. Ekert. But he forgot to stipulate three hot meals a day brought up on a platter. So somebody has to buy food while he hides out in here."

He couldn't see any reason for her huffiness, but he sighed and said, "I guess we better. Charlie needs more milk."

Tater said, "Little bastard sure eats, don't he? Got used to that grind-house food coming regular."

Yankee's head snapped around. "What did you say?"

Innocence slid across Tater's face. "Just said looks like his mama done a good job of taking care of him."

She marched over to him and smacked him in the face. He and Sammy both flinched and grinned in identical reactions. "You leave Charlie alone," she commanded, her voice soft and full of fire. "He's an innocent little boy."

Tater made his protective grin bigger. "I was just saying you could always pick a practical line of work like she done. Unless you're scared you'd get your pride bent too much."

You're sure enjoying your moment, Sammy thought. Baiting her, all earnest-looking. He was sorry to see the anger drain out of Yankee, leaving her face subdued and her eyes troubled, like his mother's. She said, "I want to have a say about who bends my pride." Her lips pressed tight in pain as she probed deep into her feelings. "I may not have control of my life, but I won't be a roller towel for just anybody who wants to use me, the way Nellie was. But I won't judge her, either. And I won't let you."

"Quit bothering her," Sammy said with unexpected heat. What was Tater trying to do—drag her down till she got to his level? He clashed the stove door loudly, getting the fire going.

Tater ignored him. "Well, you just keep making the rounds," he told her solicitously. "Somebody's bound to give you a fine honorable job cleaning their chamber pots."

Sammy yelled, "Leave her alone." She knew she was beholden to him. He didn't have to rub it in. "Don't you know when to stop?"

"Stop what?" Tater asked, letting the chips fall around his feet.

She went out, still pale. Sammy followed.

Without Charlie, they could ask for work together. They got another shoveling job. Then they cleaned out a woman's cow shed so she could store her new car. It wasn't chamber pots, but it came close.

"You and him don't hit it off too good," Sammy said.

"He rubs me wrong," Yankee said. "And scares me, I guess. I get all defensive. He's hard to like, Sammy."

"He's strutting. I guess this is the best day of his life."

"I don't know how to talk to somebody who thinks he's got a claim to fame for killing a man and burning a building. It mixes me up." They were back on the street, wondering tiredly where to try next. "What are we going to do about him? I don't like him hiding out at Mick's. Does the company suspect him or not?"

Sammy shrugged. He didn't know. To be with Tater was what mattered. He didn't want her getting any ideas about changing that.

They heard about an old couple moving away who might need help loading up their furniture, but when they got to the house it was empty. It looked sad. They went back into town. With the sun behind the peaks the cold became a blueness slowly filling with yellow windows. Stores began to close. They rushed in and spent their earnings on beans and macaroni that could be cooked, now that they had coal.

Tater was still whittling. The little links trailed over his knees. But what brought them to a colliding halt inside the door was the way he looked. He had bathed. His hair flamed in the lamplight at his shoulder. He was wearing a shirt and pants Sammy had never seen, and his own washed clothes hung dripping on the diaper line.

"Cripes, you look different," Sammy exclaimed in admiration.

Yankee braced herself. "You get out of those clothes. Those are Mick's clothes."

"Nice," Tater said, lifting the front of the shirt by a button.

Sammy saw distress twist her face up. "You get out of my brother's clothes! You stupid meddler—you can't just paw through his things."

Tater dusted the chips off his knees onto Charlie, asleep at his feet. "I was trying to get clean, Miss Doodle. I can't do nothing right to please you, can I?"

"And quit calling me that!" she commanded, feeling the soppy bottom edges of his washing. She struggled to calm herself, seeing she had barged headfirst into a dead end. His roll had been in the fire. There wasn't anything else for him to wear.

"Didn't mean to taint your keepsakes," Tater said. He almost looked like he meant it, Sammy thought, surprised.

"Just shut up," she said, hacking up salt pork to fry. "You're a smart aleck and I resent you, and as long as that's understood we might as well eat and make the best of it."

Sammy got the potatoes ready to add to the grease. The room was wonderfully warm. For the first time since he'd stepped off the train he was comfortable without his coat. Contentment settled on him. He made a little grin to match Tater's.

They ate, giving Charlie great attention so they didn't have to talk to each other. Tater remembered just in time to lick his fingers instead of wiping them on Mick's shirt, and went back to his whittling.

Yankee watched. Supper seemed to have melted her irritation. She said hesitantly, "I know I have to give up Mick's things. I started. Yesterday. I couldn't, yet, but I sent Sammy. It's just—so soon." Tater worked on, turning the delicate little snake back and forth. Finally she swallowed and said, "I never knew how that was done." Tater's mouth made a quirk of pleasure. It tickled him, Sammy could see, that she thought the chain was beautiful and couldn't say so. She said, "Don't your hands get tired?"

Tater held them out, long and bony, with pared scrubbed nails. "Sure. When I chop cotton. When I string bobwire." He turned them palm up and let her see the yellow calluses. "Not when I'm doing what I want to do."

"What's it for?" she asked.

He shrugged. "Nothing. You want it?"

She seemed to be trying to see in his eyes what he was thinking, but he bent over his work and all she got was a view of his fox-fur hair. "You have a long way to go yet," she said, and abruptly went to the ladder. From the loft she beckoned for Sammy to lift Charlie up.

Tater studied the ceiling squeaking under her footsteps. "She's took a liking to you, Sammy. Reckon what you're doing right?"

"I don't know," he murmured, baffled himself. "She'd like you if you'd give her a chance."

Tater shook his head. "Don't need the bother."

"Was you making that thing for her?" Sammy asked.

Tater said softly, "Why don't you get the hell to bed?"

Sammy went to the window. He didn't want to leave. The feeling was too good, and he was too stirred up to be sleepy. "You need to carve a little do-funny at the end. A ball-in-a-cage. She'd like that."

Tater looked at it, and his mouth made an achy droop. "Why would she?" he asked.

Sammy gazed over the black rooftops, and wondered with a thud if someone passing the ruins of the boardinghouse could still feel heat radiating from it.

His feet hurt. He guessed it was his muddy shoes drying stiff. But maybe he was outgrowing them, and they'd have to go on to Jesse. He tried to see his little brother's skewed face, but nothing came. It was hard to imagine her and the kids asleep out there somewhere, trusting them to come riding up with their pockets stuffed with money. Or Pap on his jailhouse cot, looking at the wall.

"I wish Mr. Ekert would've paid you," he said bitterly, thinking how it could have changed their lives.

"This is just the beginning," Tater said.

"What's that mean?" He felt apprehension slide through him.

"Means this morning I talked, and somebody listened. Nobody ever done that before. I liked it, Sammy." He watched the ceiling as if he'd see it change when she lay down on her mattress. "And then Mr. Ekert spieled awhile about how the strike would help out the miners, and how they could maybe win it."

"How?" Sammy asked.

"Different things. We talked about Mr. Stoker, he's the—"

"I know," Sammy said. "What about Mr. Stoker?"

"Nothing. We just mentioned him."

"You sure the company don't know it was you this morning?"

"Maybe they've guessed by now." Tater got up, stretching, and went to the door.

"Where you going? I'll go with you." In his mind he saw all the shadowy places where someone could be hiding.

"The company's not going to gun me down on my way to the outhouse," Tater said. "You get yourself up that ladder."

It was like old times, being bossed. Sammy climbed to the loft. Yankee's even breathing was strong enough to hear. He lay without moving until he heard Tater come back in. Slowly he let his gathered muscles turn loose.

He was tunneling deep down into a dream when the light glowing up through the trapdoor went out. He heard Tater climbing, and rose up through his shaft of sleep to whisper, "Over here."

A shape came toward him in the dark. Tater's voice, with a quirky lilt to it, whispered back, "There you are. I couldn't decide which bed. I had my nap on that other one."

He loomed over Sammy on the mattress. He had stripped. He had the eerie glow of a dead tree, peeled of its bark but still standing, stark and dangerous. "What are you doing?" Sammy blurted, forgetting to whisper.

"I put his clothes back in the box," Tater said. "All folded up nice."

"Cripes, just get under the cover," Sammy whispered, going rigid with shocked surprise. "You'll freeze your walleyed—" He couldn't think what to pick first.

"It ain't all that cold," Tater said. He looked around, taking his time. "With a little something in the stove for a change." Over in the Odd Fellows Hall next door, a big player organ rumbled into a ragtime march. "What's that?" he asked. "A dance place?"

"I guess so," Sammy said, holding the cover back hopefully. "Just get in."

"I bet I could dance," Tater said. "With some little fuzzy peacherine to help me, I could dance."

"Tater, come on," Sammy coaxed. He was using the voice he used on Pap, only this time he was dealing with somebody drunk on himself.

Tater crawled under the quilts, making a jerky chuckle that almost hid his shivers. He whispered, "Scoot your backporch and give me room." Sammy sagged in relief. He slowly filled himself with Tater's dark, familiar smell. They settled. Tater said idly, "What you bet she's wide awake over there, taking those nice long breaths."

"Cripes, I hope not," Sammy mumbled. "Just hush talking. How come you suddenly got to get yourself admired in the middle of the night?" Although, come to think about it, he guessed it had a better chance of working now than in daylight.

Tater made his fake chuckle. "Bet those little knobs are raising the covers up and down, up and down."

They heard her flip over, putting her back to them, so hard that she jarred a whine out of Charlie, curled beside her.

"Stop trying to wake her up like that," Sammy whispered, straining to feel whether she was asleep or pretending.

"Like what?" Tater chuckled. "What?"

Sammy turned away, too, in angry silence. The air felt different, like smooth water that was suddenly flowing over hidden rocks. He wanted to say, You're acting like a fired-up fool, but he lay quiet and cold as far as he could get from the strung-tight body that had warmed all the nights of his life.

You ruin things, he thought regretfully.

The music next door stopped. It started again, a

134

slow ragtime drag, just barely audible, with the same jaunty loneliness as Tater's laugh.

Tater said in a low voice, "Hey, Sammy. Did you see the car I got to ride in? A Packard." When there was no answer he yawned. "So guess what—it stalled and I knew what to tell the guy to do."

Sammy listened to the aching music and pressed his mouth tight.

Tater propped his arms behind his head. "Mr. Ekert said it would've been better if I'd set the fire while everybody was still in there."

"Cripes," he breathed, shocked out of his silence.

"So I said, Sure, I really *did* set it earlier, but it just didn't get burning as quick as I figured it would."

Sammy turned on his back, feeling sick. "You didn't, really, though. Did you?"

Tater made a shrug that moved the covers. "Sammy, I tell it to fit whoever's listening."

That's not what I asked, he wanted to yell. Which way did you rearrange the truth when you were telling us?

"That woman that was cooking breakfast," he said. "You warned her. You didn't want nobody hurt."

"Sure, I warned her. I told her I overheard a bunch of wops planning a fire and I just had to tell her, even if they roughed me up for it." He jerked in a laugh. "She lit out making dust."

Sammy felt the icicle-and-heat strangeness again, thinking of Yankee listening. Would he be gloating right along with Tater over his lies and schemes if she hadn't been there like new ears he was listening through?

"I told her a dinge named Bledsoe was the ring-leader—just in case she decided to tattle."

135

"Why'd you want to get him into trouble?" Sammy asked.

"Didn't like his snoopy spy ways." Tater stared at the rafters bracing each other in the dark. "Didn't like his name."

What had Yankee said on the train? Changing names won't help.

Tater stretched with careful indolence. "Anyway, I'm glad it's over with. It was a little scary. But damn, while I was doing it, I felt—" He groped tiredly for a word exciting enough. "It was the most alive I ever felt." He turned to Sammy. "I wish Pap could've saw me."

"More alive than that other time?" Sammy asked.

Tater grew still and stared at the ceiling, silent. Another rag started, just a throb they could feel through the frosty shingles above them. They listened until it stopped, and waited. But it was the last song.

Nineteen

SAMMY WOKE grabbing the cover that was being carried off by Tater's thrashing shoulders. For a second he was back again in Old Lady Chism's rent house, and Tater's voice was as raw with pain as the scars had been then. He had already caught Tater's arms before he remembered where he was.

Tater cringed and lay rigid. His hands closed on Sammy's arms like teeth. "Name of God, girl," he begged. "Don't do it!" His nightmare voice, like a plug being pulled, let his breath out in shuddering gushes. Sammy shook him. "Don't," Tater implored. "Don't do it."

Sammy threw his whole weight onto Tater's chest. "Wake up," he urged softly. "I'm here. Tater. It's me."

He felt the knotted muscles under him drop slack. Only the hands kept holding him, stroking shakily, testing his reality.

"I'm here. It's all right." He moved off Tater's chest. Even in the dark he knew to take the edge of the quilt and wipe the cold sweat from his face. He covered them both, and lay listening to Tater's thudding heart.

"What did I say?" Tater whispered in his daytime voice.

Sammy hesitated. He didn't see how Yankee could still be asleep, but maybe she was. "Something about a girl. You said, 'Don't, girl.'"

He could hear Tater wetting his dry mouth. "She had that rope around me again."

"What rope?"

Tater's head slowly rocked, erasing the nightmare. "Nothing. No rope. I was dreaming crazy." He raised his head and peered into the dark.

"Dreaming about the fire?" Sammy knew who he was checking. "No, she's asleep. She sleeps deep, really deep. You didn't wake her up." It didn't matter if she was listening wide-eyed or not. It mattered that Tater was talking to him. "Was you dreaming about the night you got hurt?"

Tater's head rocked again. "Can't tell you," he whispered.

"But why?" Sammy waited. "It's like pus in there, Tater. You can't heal."

"Thought she was going to string me up." Tater made a sniff of sound, to belittle the idea.

"Who?" Then he thought he knew. "Ben Sills's girl?"

"The scary part was, half of me was trying to wake up, and half of me was trying to go on dreaming till she done it."

Sammy felt tremors start in him. He was going to know the rest of it now. How it had really happened. Why. He said carefully, "I never understood how it went, exactly. That night." The picture opened in his mind again, always the same: Old Lady Chism's rangeland empty to the horizon, with a wagon track wandering through it like a string. And the girl, clearer than he wanted. The crinkled hair. The eyes searching. As round as the day he had smashed the lunch pail she offered him. "She went looking for her pap when he didn't come home. I could figure that. But how come she found you?" His chest had an anvil on it.

"When she found him, he'd already found me," Tater whispered. "I got dragged a long ways, when Pap's horse bolted."

Sammy's ears began to thud. Bam. He couldn't stop it. Bam. He saw Pap's spooked old pegger give a lurch that threw Tater but left his foot caught in the stirrup as they crashed off through the brush.

"But how could he follow along and find you? I thought you'd already—he was shot by then."

"A jig's tough," Tater said. "I guess he crawled."

Sammy eased over to the cold edge of the mattress. He wished all he had wondered about had stayed puzzle pieces and never fitted together to be real.

"Then she come and found you both?"

Tater's straw pillow rustled as he nodded. "She seen his fire. He fixed a little fire, and covered me up. She brought his wagon down to where we was. He got hisself in. I couldn't. So she throwed Pap's ketch rope over a limb and under my arms, to help me. But I thought—" He broke off, drawing long memory-blocking breaths.

"What? That she meant to hang you?"

"She could have. Or run the wagon over me. Anything. Or just left me. I couldn't have made it to no help."

"But she didn't. She brought you home."

"Even Pap's horse," Tater said levelly. "She even chased it down and brought it, too. Crazy. With him lying there in the wagon." Sammy heard him swallowing a taste that wouldn't go down. "But before she come was the worst part, that whole night and next day. Part of the time I was passed out. But he'd still be sitting there by me. And I'd wake up and think, 'Just die!'"

They studied the rafters. A train passed a crossing far away. Then a closer crossing, with the same four lonesome sounds.

"Why couldn't I made a good clean shot?" Tater whispered. "He stood up. He asked me was I lost. Could he help me. Why couldn't I made a fast clean shot right then?"

The train came closer, and screeched with icy clarity at the first crossroads of town. Sammy flinched in spite of himself.

"God, he lasted," Tater said. "Looking at me."

"I didn't know that part," Sammy said dimly.

They listened to the train come in, trembling with power.

"You could've pretty well guessed it, though, couldn't you?"

Sammy rubbed his stinging eyes. "No. How? You never told me. I wasn't there. You didn't let me be in on it. Why was that? I thought we done everything together. But you took off out into nowhere after him, all by yourself. Why wasn't I there?"

To be guilty with you, he added in his heart. To stop you. Or help you. Whichever I would have done.

He lay motionless, afraid to think which he would have chosen.

Tater said, "Then he did. Did die. Before I got in the wagon. Because when she tugged me over on

140

his bedroll, we was side by side. Him dead, and me thinking I was next, highballing right for hell. And it wasn't going to help me a bit that he was just a—just a—"

Sammy said, "Jesus, Tater. Why'd you do it?" His throat felt scalded. "He stood up. He was coming towards you."

In the silence Charlie made a cry, and slept on.

"I thought it'd help," Tater said.

"How could you think that? He had a wife and four kids." Behind his eyes Sammy saw Ben Sills and his children going past him in the road, carrying each other along.

"Help *me*, maybe," Tater said. "To know I could do it. Do something." He was silent again. "I thought it might make me different. Like maybe bigger. But it didn't, I guess. I guess doing it's the easy part, just the beginning." He thrashed restlessly in the dark. "Now sometimes I wish the law would just take me. Just fry me and get it over with. But I guess that's too easy, too. You don't get to just die."

Sammy stared at the rafters in a stillness like the moment before they ran for the delivery wagon, a choosing moment. He said, "But there's got to be reasons, big reasons. What had he done to you?"

Tater dragged his fingers through his clean hair. "I wanted us to get our turn, and he was the one I saw getting on ahead of us and leaving us in the hole—"

"That's not enough!" Sammy said in despair.

I was depending on your *reasons,* he almost yelled. That's what makes it so terrible—that there wasn't any Godamighty-it's-either-me-or-you reason, and you did it because you wanted to.

"He hadn't hurt you," he said. "Cripes, he maybe

saved your life. He didn't have to stay there, taking care of you."

"I didn't want him saving me, damn it," Tater said. "That's what messed me up. Her carrying me home like that, and him—if he could've just died and let it be over, instead of making me think about it. He wasn't supposed to come crawling after me!"

The train started up. Each chuff of the engine was like a gasp. Try. Try. Try. Until it was moving, going on.

Tater said, "Damn it, it's like I got this chance, now. Like they give me back this life. You know? And what am I doing with it. I thought I'd do something with it. But I just go on being the way I was. I wanted something better to happen."

Sammy struggled with a revelation he couldn't find the words for. He thought, All that time, while he sat there keeping you alive—that was showing you something better. Jesus. It was. And you still don't see it.

Unexpectedly Tater jerked in a silent laugh. "Even this, today. It's a pretty good joke." His voice flattened out. "I thought I was coming over to the good side. Over with you, and her, and her holy miners. But what they want me for is their dirty work."

"You don't have to do nobody's dirty work."

"Except that's where the money is, Sammy. Hell, if they got more work for me, I want it."

"No you don't," he protested. "You don't."

"I can do it." Tater turned away, carrying the cover off Sammy's taut knees. "It grows on you. You know? After a while it's like with a girl you want. Doing it's all you think about."

In the silence Sammy felt a bond between them break and dump him slowly into emptiness. He almost reached out his hand to test the space where the part of him that had worshiped without judgment and accepted without question had been.

Tater whispered, "Hey, I'm cold."

Sammy felt an arm arch over him and pull him close. He lay like a sickle, resisting, curved to Tater's hard shape, until he felt him sag like Pap at the end of a liquoring and jolt exhausted into sleep.

Twenty

IN THE MORNING Tater was gone. Sammy sat up with such a start that Charlie, crawling along Yankee's shoulder, jumped and toppled over on her face. As she woke and untangled him, Sammy slid out of bed and down the ladder. He didn't feel like meeting her eyes.

Tater was whittling, slouched in his own clean, dry clothes. The desk, where his wood chips were falling, was covered with food. Bread and sausages and canned peaches and sardines were piled around sacks and boxes Sammy couldn't make out. Five shiny red apples sat in a row.

Tater looked up past him and said, "Take the kid before she drops him on his head."

Sammy made a wheeze of surprise, and swung Charlie to the floor. Yankee climbed down and stood beside him, silently staring. Finally she said, "What are we supposed to think? Stores aren't open yet." She drew herself up, determined and cold. "If you stole that stuff it has to go back."

"You take your part back, Miss Doodle," Tater said, standing up in a rain of whittlings. The stove was hot. He handed her a long sausage and put three others into the skillet.

"That was some haul," Sammy said uncertainly.

"It has to go back," Yankee said. "You can't break into a store and take food."

It felt odd to Sammy not to be pelting Tater with questions about how he'd done it. Was it last night that made him feel strained? Or the fire? Or all the changes together that had caused Tater to take on as many shades of gray as the mountains lapping one over the other beyond the window?

The sausages sizzled. He watched, trying not to look hungry. Charlie climbed Tater's leg, making hopeful jabber. "This is my house," Yankee said louder because no one was listening. "I don't do things this way." Sammy felt sorry for her, standing there with her raw sausage, helpless to stop what was offending her sense of rightness.

Tater brushed her aside to stir flour in the grease and add canned milk to make gravy. "Don't eat, then," he said. "Don't feed the kid neither if you think my kind of food'll rot his gut."

"Stop making fun of me," she exclaimed. "Stop belittling all the things I believe in." She threw the sausage at him, and missed.

He said, "I was out there risking my fool neck for this. Who's cutting down who? You could tell me thanks for trying."

"Nobody asked you to risk your neck!"

"Nobody's asking you to eat what I brought." He went to the desk and scraped everything off of it with one sweep. Cans clattered and rolled across the floor.

Tater set plates where the food had been, stepping

145

on the fallen mess. Sammy looked down at it, suddenly seeing himself holding out a pork chop. Can't you be proud of me? I done it for you. He picked up the bruised apples and dented cans. A bag of beans had broken. Charlie gathered some to chew on.

Yankee knelt and scooped them into the hem of her skirt. Sammy saw her face crumpling as she cried. He crawled around the desk legs hunting the strays, and silently filled the empty wardrobe shelves with beautiful immoral food.

She stood at the window with her back to them. Tater filled his plate and ate. Sammy filled his. He felt like Reba's doll being pulled two ways. He looked at Yankee's bent shoulders. Slowly he halved his sausage and put it with gravy and bread on another plate.

When he handed it to her she shook her head. She looked past it at Charlie on Tater's knee getting gravy spooned into his mouth. "He wanted to do something to help," Sammy said, struggling to decide if what Tater had done was wrong, or right, or both. He found the raw sausage, wiped it, and put it on to cook. "But it was too risky," he told Tater stiffly. "If you'd got caught we'd be in trouble."

"Damn near did," Tater said, chopping Charlie's sausage with the side of his fork. "In the alley a bunch of guys sneaked right by me, heading somewhere really fast and quiet."

"See? That might have been the company looking for you."

"Sammy, that's dumb. I'm not worth sending a hunting party out for." He mopped his plate. "But okay, I won't go no more. You bring in the next haul."

Sammy looked around, hunting along the walls for strength. "I'd rather do it her way. Getting a job

146

and paying for things with my own money. You done something we needed, and it took nerve, but—"

"But some of Miss Good's high-mindedness is beginning to rub off on you? Right?"

"She *is* good," he said.

"Where's it got her?" Tater asked.

They watched Yankee drag on her coat and go out the door, her face tight with determination, to look for work.

"Off to set the world on fire," Tater said.

Sammy got his own coat and went down into the rutted street. Yankee was already out of sight. He pivoted, feeling bristly and hopeless. There weren't any jobs. But he couldn't go back in there and eat stolen food after what he'd said. He set his shoulders and started up the canyon road to Back Town.

The thought of the darkness scared him. He remembered the mules. He dreaded to walk past miners who had put their jobs and maybe even their lives on the line for the things the union was trying to get for them. But he was going up to the mine to ask for work.

I can do something without you, he told Tater.

He was passing Mr. Stoker's big house before he realized it. Smoke came from the tall chimneys. A car stood waiting below the long front porch. Mr. Stoker came clumping down the steps, stubby in his thick fur coat, and yanked open the car door before the bundled-up driver had time to spring out and do it for him.

A small, round-cheeked girl ran to the edge of the porch. "Bye, Papa," she called, swinging by one arm from a porch post. She wore little red shoes. "I love you, Papa."

Mr. Stoker's head came out of the car. "I love you, too, pet," he answered over the engine's rumble. The car bucked off, nearly stalling before it finally crunched along the drive and headed uphill toward the mine.

Sammy backed into the ditch to let it pass. He hadn't known people shouted words like that publicly. A woman in a black dress took the little girl's waving hand and led her inside.

He wished he hadn't been passing. He didn't want Mr. Stoker to be a father, or loving, or anything but the powerful, stubborn rich-men's man who wouldn't let the miners have their rights.

Up the slope he could see the windows of the tallest mine buildings glinting above an ugly gray sprawl of houses. He wondered which house Yankee had lived in, when she was the size of that little girl. Which ash heap had she stood on, to look down on Pegler and the plains and the train tracks escaping into the hazy rest of the world?

He puffed around another curve and found himself facing a tall fence with a gate. A group of men stood outside it, making a low, long sound like a tumble of rocks. At a building inside the fence, five armed men stood watching. With a little start he saw a man with a rifle crouched on a water tower up nearer the mine.

Some of the miners began to push the gate back and forth. Someone inside shouted, "Sure, break it open. Come on in—we're ready for you." The miners yelled back, pushing harder.

Sammy eased into the edge of the group. "How do I get in there?" he asked. No one heard him. "I want to work here," he said above the shouts.

Someone at his side said, "You better leave, kid. A couple of our boys are hurt in there."

The miners quieted as someone inside the gate called through a horn, "Your men are being sent out. Break up. If you start anything—*anything*—they'll never get past this gate."

A wagon came around one of the dark buildings at the mine. Inside and outside the gate, men stepped out of the road to clear a way. The gate was opened. The wagon creaked through. Two men in bloody clothes sat in the back between two armed guards. Another guard sat with the driver, bent over his rifle like a trap ready to snap.

"What did they do?" Sammy begged somebody.

A man beside him said, "The tipple got dynamited last night. Them two didn't get away."

"But are they taking them to the doctor—"

"Jail," the man said. He made a long racking cough. "Unless we can change their plans." Without warning he leaped toward the guard beside the driver. The guard kicked out and sent the man blundering back into the crowd that had suddenly surrounded the wagon. The two guards in the back began to swing at the miners grabbing for them.

A shot went zinging over Sammy's head, eerily whining into space. He felt himself lifted off the ground and shoved into the back of the wagon. The driver gave a whoop that sent the horses clattering down the road. Miners fell away, dragging a guard out with them.

Sammy righted himself, jolting wildly. Men from inside the gate were rushing out into the welter of bodies. A gun came up out of the fighting mass and cracked down on a head.

"Jesus," he breathed, thinking of Yankee's geodes.

The wagon swept around a curve that hid everything. It rattled over rocks and ruts in a bone-cracking rush. One of the injured men pitched forward. Blood trickled from his ear.

Sammy's stomach began to churn. The wagon

slowed a little, because no one had followed. Sammy looked at the two wounded men, thinking of the silent shapes Tater had seen in the alley.

Was that you? he thought. All fired up to pull off something big? And now you're on your way to jail. And that's where Tater's headed, if he's caught like you.

They passed someone standing by the road at the edge of town.

"Wait—let me off!" he cried, realizing it had been Yankee, but the wagon lumbered on. He jumped, staggered a few buckling steps, and hit the slush nose-first. Yankee ran to help him wobble to his feet.

She gasped, "I knew it. I just had the feeling you went up there."

"There's trouble at the gate," he said when he got his voice working. "They made me come back down—"

"In town they're saying strikers blew up the tipple early this morning. The company's calling in twenty more deputies to guard the buildings." She tried to brush mud from his front. "Two hurt men are still in there."

"No, that's them," Sammy said. "Going to jail."

"Oh, Sammy, I'm glad you're back. I don't want you up there!" All at once she squeezed him in a hug.

"Hey," he protested, as her anxious mouth bumped his cheek.

She let him step back, still holding him, concerned. "Look at you, you little skinny weasel. You can't work there. You've got to stay up in the light, Sammy."

He had never been grabbed close like that before. It caught him off guard.

"What you doing here?" he asked when he could, fighting the flush of pleasure spreading over his face and neck. "Did you find work?"

She started toward the middle of town. "No. But I found you."

At a side street she stuck out her hand to stop him. A little funeral procession was coming toward them. They let the mourners walk by in their old-country clothes. The women's sodden skirts trailed in the mud. Two men carried a coffin the size of a little trunk.

Yankee watched with her lips pressed tight. He wondered if she was thinking of Mick and the strike and all its high hopes. Or Miss Blue, or Mr. Stoker's little girl in her other world. Or Charlie safe in a warm room.

He waited for her to walk on, when the procession ended, but he saw that her gaze had lifted to the dingy row of shacks away off across the train tracks, where one of the girls, in a flouncy wrapper, was sweeping her steps, *whish whish whish*, like a tiny windup doll.

He took her chapped hand and started her home.

Mr. Ekert's car was in front of the barbershop. A man stood by it in a dark overcoat, rocking on his heels.

Twenty-one

TATER OPENED THE DOOR as they climbed up.

"I told him I'd have to wait till somebody got here to watch the kid," he said, passing them on the landing. He got into the car so quickly they only stared.

They went inside. Charlie was dropping Tater's closed-up pocketknife in and out of a tin cup.

"What do you think?" Yankee asked anxiously. Her breakfast plate, covered with a second dish, was waiting on the desk. Slowly she ate her sausage.

"Mr. Ekert wants him for another job," Sammy said, feeling dread.

"Mick said Mr. Ekert was like that. He gets his fly-by-night jobs done by some roughneck kid raring to prove how tough he is, then throws him away." She opened a can of sardines and made him a sandwich. A tail hung out of it. He didn't think he could eat it.

"Let him throw," he said with an ache in his throat, almost believing he meant it. I don't feel anything, he told Tater. I don't hurt for you no more.

She said gently, "I'm sorry for the way it's gone, Sammy. Last night—that was sad."

"Did you hear everything?"

She nodded, feeding Charlie mashed sardines.

"Why can't he be sorry?" he asked. "Why can't he regret? I give up on him till he comes to his senses. I give up."

"Oh, Sammy, no." She knocked the little wooden chain off the back of the chair, and nervously hung it up again. "If *you* wait to do the right thing till *he* does, how will you ever start? You have to do it as if you expected him to follow along."

"*You* try expecting him," he dared her. "Try it. You can't. You don't like him. Try telling him you like him. He likes you. He wants you to like him, so bad it galls him."

A flush spread over her face. He couldn't tell if it came from surprise or anger. She wiped sardine oil off of Charlie. "When you told me, on the train, about what he did—all I could see was that other man aiming a gun at Mick. After Mick—" She closed her eyes. "I hated that man. The first days after Mick got killed, I swore I was going to make that man pay. If it took the rest of my life." She turned abruptly and gathered diapers to wash. "When Tate came—" She tried to think. "And there he was, right before my eyes, somebody real with needs and lacks and all those bent reasons for doing what he did—"

Sammy strained so hard to grasp what she was getting at that he ate the tail of his sandwich without thinking. "Tater didn't kill Mick," he said.

"But he made me see how somebody did. And I didn't like that. When you begin to understand somebody . . ." Her troubled eyes lifted to Sammy. "But I have to find a way to live with that man walking free, don't I? I do. Or else he's taking my life, too. Along with Mick's."

Sammy gazed out at the snowy mountains. For the first time he let himself look at the horror Yankee saw in her memory, and would never get over and had to live with, like Tater and his scars. Before he could stop, another face filled his mind, the round black face of Ben Sills's girl, who would never get over Tater.

Yankee said, "Maybe if I tell myself what killed Mick was like a lightning bolt, or black lung, that I wouldn't try to get revenge for—maybe I can live with that."

Did you call him lightning? he asked Ben Sills's girl. How did you block him off, so you could stand it, and go on living?

Mick's body had lain in this room, Sammy suddenly remembered. Next day she'd had to walk back and forth across the spot. She'd scrubbed the blood, maybe. He had a stabbing urge to comfort her for that day. Reach and hold her the way she had held him when he came down from Back Town.

She sliced big curls from a bar of lye soap, and patted Charlie's diapers down into the sudsy water. She said, "It looked like they were planning a supper at the Methodist church when I went by. I thought we might get jobs helping to clean up." She studied his face. "But you want to be here when he gets back."

"Yes," he said faintly. "I'll watch Charlie."

Charlie cried when she left. Because they were alone, Sammy smoothed his hair and carried him up and down, making little hum-songs until he went to sleep. He held him, sitting in Mick's big chair, feel-

154

ing foreboding grow in him like the heavy clouds that had made a second range of mountains in the west. The sun dropped behind them, and the town turned the colors of ice.

Finally, Tater came in. He shook down the ashes and put more coal in the stove without looking at Sammy. His face was taut. He put his cold hands on either side of the stovepipe as if he might close his fingers around it.

"What did he want?" Sammy finally burst out.

Tater touched the hot metal with his fingertips. "If he'd wanted you to kow, he would've invited you along, Sammy."

"Don't give me that," Sammy exclaimed. "He wants you to pull something off."

Tater's scarred eyebrow cocked, questioning him.

"Yankee says he's using you. Then there's trouble, and suddenly he never saw you before."

"He'll remember me," Tater said.

"What does he want you to do?"

Tater made a stiff laugh. "I can't tell you that! He just wants anything big enough to give those New York high-ups a scare. And he says there's times when somebody that nobody's expecting can do the job better than some expert."

"Mr. Stoker," Sammy said. "That big?" He watched Tater's face slowly shut again like a door. "Last night you said you two talked about Mr. Stoker."

"He talked. I listened. There's money in it this time, though, Sammy. A lot of money."

"For killing Mr. Stoker?" His voice slanted up in disbelief. "You can't do that—he's the head man. You'll end up dead."

"Or rich, one or the other."

"Jesus—don't say that, Tater," he begged, so convulsively that Charlie stirred in his arms with a cry. "Say you won't. Say you're not even thinking about it."

"But I'm thinking about it."

It was like being in a dream. "You've already decided, haven't you?" It was like being caught in a hole so tight his arms couldn't move. "You can't just decide something that terrible! You're talking about people's lives! That can't never be changed back the way they were." He strained to free himself and wake up. "You told Pap you done what you done for him, and maybe you thought you had a good enough reason, but you didn't. You didn't help nothing. You still got to work out a way to live with how things are. And with Mr. Stoker you wouldn't have no reason but money."

"Money's a help when the hurting takes hold," Tater said.

"You're *supposed* to hurt sometimes! So you won't do the same things again." He got to his feet, fighting to say it right because it mattered so much. "It's like—like sticking your hand in the fire. It's supposed to hurt you into looking ahead, and being scared for next time."

"I'm not that dumb," Tater said.

"You are, damn it—you do things wham-bang, without ever picturing ahead to see if you might be sorry."

"She's sure been working on you, Sammy."

He closed his eyes. His dream voice wasn't getting through. "No, sometimes I figure out things by myself," he said wearily. He watched Tater get a can of beans from the wardrobe and hack off the lid with the can opener. "Mr. Stoker has a little girl."

"Does he? Not a bit different from your little sisters, I bet. Same ragged clothes and hungry look, right?"

They held each other's gaze like arm wrestlers straining in silent balance. Sammy looked away.

"How come she gets that kind of life and they don't?" Tater asked softly. "Or Jesse don't? Or me? Don't we deserve some of that?"

He looked at Tater's body strung like a bow that was aiming its deadly intention out at somebody. "Everybody does," he said desperately. "But some better way. You're not Jesse—you got reasoning!"

Tater found a fork and stabbed into his beans. He said, "I don't know no other way to get listened to."

"You could find a way. You don't want to. That takes facing up to your life—"

"Hell, Sammy, this is my life. I've blowed stumps and butchered hogs and took whippings till that's what I know. It's what I can do."

"Then do it different," he begged. "You get to make choices. Change—it's all right to change!"

Tater chewed and looked at him. Sammy's own mouth felt like dry leather. Helplessness made him dizzy. It was like babies coming. It was like Bam. One of the going-to-happen things that nothing could stop.

But he had to try. "I don't think—" he began, struggling. "That man you killed—I don't think he saved your life so you could do another wrong thing."

"Leave it alone, Sammy," Tater warned.

"You don't want to do better. You want to do what you damn please and bet on God forgiving you because you had the guts to spit in his eye."

Tater pried open the back window and pitched his empty can into the alley. "Sammy, I'm just half a mile from hell already. Don't you figure he's already wrote me off?"

Sammy blinked his eyes against the nettle-sting of tears. "I don't know," he whispered. He stared out the window as though he could see the words' vibrations rising over the rooftops to the sky.

When he looked around, Tater had slung on his coat and was going out the door.

"Oh, Jesus—no," he yelled. "I'm coming with you." He rattled down the stairs.

Tater turned on him. "Get the kid back up there. You want him froze?"

Sammy looked down at Charlie crushed round-eyed and forgotten in his arms. "Wait for me," he gasped. "I'll wrap him up. Wait—"

Tater walked away in the twilight.

Charlie let out a howl that Sammy felt in his own throat. He saw Tater step off the curb at the corner, then step back up, staring at something down a side street. He ran to where Tater stood. At first all he saw was a little group of people with bundles. Going back to the old country, his mind said. Then he felt a flash of heat rush through him in the cold dusk.

Yankee was hurrying toward them. Behind her, slower, crowded in a tired huddle, came his mother and the kids.

Twenty-two

"I KNEW who they were," Yankee exclaimed as she reached them. "When I passed the depot, and they were standing there, looking lost—" Charlie stretched his arms for her, bawling. She took him, and said over his head, "I turned around and went up to them. I said, I know you."

Reba was tugging Colleen along. Jesse carried Pearl. Their mother stopped in front of Tater with Pap's bedroll in her arms. He said, "How in tarnation—" His eyes flicked back up the street they had come down. "Is Pap with you? Is he out?"

Such a shadow crossed her face that Sammy put out his hands. For the first time in his life his mother walked into his arms, and he felt her stiffness suddenly break into little tremors. "Are you sick?" he asked.

"No," she said, almost too low to hear.

Reba opened her mouth. "Pap—" she began.

"No," her mother said.

Yankee urged them along the sidewalk. "It's warm

up there. Come. We've got food." Her eyes slid over Tater's face.

Tater stopped his mother at the foot of the stairs. "Where's Pap?" he asked.

She started up the steps in silence. But Jesse said, "Hunged. You know? Hunged." He tipped his head sharply, and popped his tongue out.

Tater hit him. "God—don't joke with me!" He slung Sammy's hands off. "What are you blabbing about?"

His mother said quietly, "He done it in jail. With the ticking from his bed. Tore into little strips. They found him."

Sammy took a gulp of cold air and held to the stair rail. He felt the blood leave his face. Up above him, Yankee, with Charlie on her hip, helped his mother climb the steps. He saw that he had to take the same steps, up through shock and horror and piercing regret, to get to the numbness of the landing. He took Pearl from Jesse, and started up.

His mother said, "She rather not keep us no more. Mrs. Unger. She paid our ways. We got on the wrong train and had to wait." She looked around, lost again, and her voice broke like glass. "She said did I want to send for you boys to come back, or use the money to come on where you was."

Potter's field, Sammy thought. Up there with Miss Blue.

His mother turned on the landing, looking out past them. She drew herself straight. "I decided," she said in little glassy splinters of sound. "I said I'd use it for coming on. Not for going back."

She let Yankee lead her inside. Sammy set Pearl down and pushed them all into the warm room. When he turned for Tater he saw him still standing at the bottom of the stairs.

"We got to go in," he said dimly.

Tater started off down the street.

Sammy rushed in and grabbed his coat, and darted out past their startled faces. He crashed through a group of people going into the Odd Fellows Hall, and ran after Tater hitching off into the twilight.

"Come back," he called. He caught up. "Tater—it's Pap. You can't just walk off!"

"I got a job," Tater said. His voice had gone as cold and empty as the unlighted buildings they were passing. "I'm due somewhere."

"Where?"

"Go back, Sammy."

"Where you due?"

"Tell her I want to be by myself, or something."

"No. I'm going with you."

Tater caught his coat and pasted him against a wall. "Sammy, this is something I'm going to do! Pap being dead don't change it. Get back up there with everybody and have a good cry."

"Come cry too," Sammy whispered.

"Not for somebody that give up on us." He limped on, under streetlights that flared across his ashy face. Sammy hovered at his side. "Not for a coward that couldn't hold out to take care of his family."

You're hurting, Sammy thought. Don't you know you are?

Tater said, "How'd he think she could manage, after he used her up?" He swerved around a corner. "She can't manage."

"She decided," Sammy said hopefully, shivering. "You heard her say. She never done that before."

"God, he couldn't stand me being free and getting away, could he? He had to go me one better." He turned into a narrow alley still crusted with snow.

"What did he want? For me not to never get out from under the load neither? Name of God, how could he do that?"

Sammy groped in his mind for something to answer. But all he could think was, Did we cause it? Was it what we done? He began to shake so hard his teeth made little clicks.

Tater stopped at the back of a thick-walled building. Steps led down to a dark basement door. He took one step down and said coldly, "This is as far as you go. The union keeps supplies down there. Somebody's waiting for me."

"What are you getting, down there?" Sammy asked. It was all still a dream he was in by mistake, endless. "A gun? Dynamite?"

"You beat it now, Sammy."

"For Mr. Stoker?" He stretched out his hands in desperation. "You don't have to prove nothing to Pap no more! He let you free to do things your own way now. You don't have to go down there."

Tater took three more steps. "What do I do when the first kid says, I'm hungry?"

"You yell back, I didn't kill a man."

Tater went to the bottom where the smoke-stained snow had drifted. He was a blur with a raspy voice that said, "Move on."

Sammy walked out of sight and stood behind an ash dump. The door to the basement opened and closed so quietly he hardly heard it. He wished he could lie down on the ground like Jesse and silently bang his head until somebody stopped him.

He didn't know what to do. Maybe Tater was a board already too warped and split and ruined for anything but burning.

He began to cry in the dark. In his mind Pap lay on his cot, staring up till he found the right beam or nail. He slung the image away, like the tears on his jaws. He thought of all they hadn't done or said when they left him yelling through the bars. It was so easy to see, now, why Pap had lashed out in anger. Tater was taking off to show the world and try himself. But Pap was staying behind, stuck with kids to feed and mean jobs and her always sick and silent, when what he craved was to strike out on a big red cutting horse back into the young, free days before everything had fences.

So maybe that's what he done, Sammy thought.

He saw Tater come slowly up out of the dark and go down the alley. He caught up and matched strides through the frozen slush.

"Jesus," Tater said in exasperation. "Go home!"

His hands were empty. He pounded them together in the cold. Sammy felt a spurt of hope. "You didn't get nothing back there."

Tater unbuttoned his coat. A short length of rope hung around his neck, and something long was tied to each end of it.

"What is that?" Sammy whispered.

Tater said softly, "Twelve-gauge shotgun, sawed off. Broke down, the barrel over here and the stock over here." He buttoned his coat over them again, and brought something from his pocket. "Shells."

"Please don't," Sammy whispered. "Please. You'll have to leave. Tonight. You'll be on the run. You can't get away with this one."

"Nix on the talk," Tater warned him, glancing cautiously around.

"I won't see you no more. You'll have to hide. You're not holding out no better than Pap. You're throwing your life away the same as him."

Tater went on to the end of the alley. A string of wagons and buggies were passing, from some meeting that had broken up. A little sullen group of miners stood on the corner.

"I'll stop you, someway," Sammy said as they dodged across the rutted street. "I'll warn Mr. Stoker."

"No you won't," Tater said.

"I will. You already killed one man nobody warned."

Suddenly Tater wasn't beside him. Sammy whirled, amazed. He was all alone. He leaped out of a wagon's way, and almost stepped in front of a car coming from the opposite direction. People passed on the sidewalks. Some laughing drunks teetered out of a saloon. But Tater, with the scornful ease that had always been magic to Sammy, had disappeared.

The unexpectedness of it left him openmouthed. He spun around again, trying to spot Tater. He had been right there! And now he was standing in one of the dark slits between buildings, or behind shadowy stairs.

"Do it, then!" he shouted at the shadows. "Do it!"

Here I am like always, trying to stay right on your heels.

A buggy nudged him out of the street. He ran along the sidewalk, peering into doorways, but Tater was gone, and there was no way to find him if he didn't want to be found. Sammy stopped, trying to think. Had someone told Tater where to find Mr. Stoker? At a meeting? Or was he on his way up to Mr. Stoker's house?

Sammy stepped out, trembly with desperation, into the path of a woman going by. "Where's the sheriff's office?" he asked.

She pointed down a street, sidestepping him, and

hurried on. Sammy started off the way she had pointed.

I got to do this, he explained to the shadows. By myself, for my own reasons. Not through you any longer. Not following.

He realized he wasn't running. Should he be running? He made his heavy feet go faster, not sure.

Twenty-three

SAMMY PASSED under the jail's high, barred windows. A light burned in an office next to it. Through the glass in the door he could see a man reading at a desk. He tried to push in. The door was locked. The man looked up and motioned him away. He banged on the door until the man rose and came to peep through the glass at him.

Sammy drew an aching breath. "My brother's going to kill somebody. Stop him."

The man slowly pulled a green shade down.

"Listen to me!" Sammy implored him, rattling the knob.

There was silence. He gave the door a kick that bruised his toes. There was only silence again, sliced in two by the far-off whistle of a train. He limped on. Who could help? Mr. Ekert? He reversed himself and hobbled as fast as he could to the union hall. The windows were dark. The door was locked.

He headed back to the street where Tater had disappeared, to start over somehow. His toes throbbed.

He thought of the morning he had run through the snow, not aware of pain.

At the canyon road a draft rushing downhill set him shivering. The sky had grown heavy. He saw a little light beckoning and hiding, like the ones in ghost stories. I got to go up there, he thought in dread. I got to check. Then he realized the light was a car winding slowly into town. He bobbed into a deep doorway as it passed. All his muscles sprang tight as he saw it was the car Mr. Stoker had ridden off in that morning, on his way to Back Town.

He ran after it as it rumbled over the crosshatched ruts. It turned out of sight, but he lunged on and saw its black top again, far ahead. It turned another corner. He sprinted, hit an ice patch that sent him sprawling, and floundered on. The car had stopped in front of the depot. The driver had opened the door.

Oh, don't! he gasped silently, running harder. Mr. Stoker helped a woman out of the car. Sammy braced to hear a shotgun blast as his eyes darted everywhere. Mr. Stoker lifted out a large suitcase. The little girl slid out of the back seat. Sammy cringed as they walked into the light of the waiting-room window. The train was pulling in.

Oh, hurry, he begged them in his mind. Get on. Just get on. He stared into every dark space between buildings. His eyes swept along the copings and turrets of any rooftop where Tater could be hiding. Bam. Oh, please just *hurry*.

He saw them walk along the platform and pass from sight behind the engine. He slowed to a shamble, his taut muscles slackening in relief. He's getting away from you, he told Tater. You missed your chance. He forced himself still, holding the pain in his side.

The whistle suddenly blasted through the wind that was drawing flakes of snow out of the dark like white sparks. The train began to move. He was so glad, he made a groan of thankfulness. Then he saw Mr. Stoker standing alone on the platform, with his hand raised.

Good-bye, Papa. I love you.

"Oh, Jesus—get on," he whispered. "You can't do that!" He began to run toward him, making his jolting voice shout, "Mr. Stoker!" But the rumble of the train drowned it.

Mr. Stoker walked to his car. The driver swung the door open and slammed it shut. The engine was running. The car made a tight circle. Its light swept Sammy as he leaped out to stop it. His hand caught a fender, but the car swerved around him and roared off up the canyon road.

He took a gulp of icy air and started after it. From the edge of town he could see the blurred lights fading away. For all he knew, Tater was already there at Mr. Stoker's fine big house, waiting for the car to pull up at the front door.

Snow was falling in a white gloom where the hills should have been. The road was already dusted with it. He ran like a jig toy in little spurts of stiffness with his eyes slitted against the snow pricks and his hand over his nose to cut the cold.

When he couldn't run he walked. The rasp of his steps hitting rocks and hollows was the only sound. He found himself against the wire of a fence. The barbs took sharp nicks from his grabbing hands before he could swerve off in the right direction and run on.

Forgive me, he whispered. Forgive me. I got to do this. He stopped, bent, clutching his side, and forced himself straight again. He threw back his head to the sky, and his cracked voice yelled, "No—to hell with forgiving me. This is right and you're wrong!"

He went on. The road strained around curves until in the distance he saw the small yellow square of a window. Mr. Stoker was home. But in the light he was a target. Sammy ran closer as another light appeared in an upstairs room. A shadow crossed the curtained window, and he jerked himself tight, tensed for the shot out of the dark.

The car stood snow-covered, black and white, at the front door. He raced past it and stumbled across the yard to the back steps. He pounded the kitchen door with both hands.

The door opened halfway. All of Sammy's strength dropped out of him. He looked up into the dark face of the man who had stopped them at the boarding-house. Bledsoe.

"Well, hello, there," the face said, and craned to glance beyond him.

"I got to see Mr. Stoker," Sammy said in a skidding voice.

Bledsoe let him into a room as warm as washwater. Without warning he caught Sammy's arm and unbuttoned his coat. His big hands patted Sammy's pockets and felt along his legs. "Who sent you, peanut?" he asked in his velvet voice.

"Nobody." He began to shake uncontrollably. "My brother's going to kill Mr. Stoker. Tell him. Warn him."

Bledsoe folded Sammy effortlessly into a chair and glanced past the hanging lamp at the ceiling. "He's busy up there. But he'll be down. Then we'll see if he wants to be bothered with this."

"Bothered?" Sammy exclaimed. "Tater could be outside that window!" He clamped his mouth shut.

He didn't know what he was doing. He was crazy. He was handing Tater over to the enemy.

Out in the hall someone came down squeaky stairs. A voice said, "Who came in?"

Bledsoe said, "We got a little problem here, Mr. Stoker."

A man came to the kitchen door. He was smaller without his pony-skin coat. His tired eyes pricked Sammy's skin. He said, "What's your name?"

Sammy stared at him, struck dumb.

"Haney," Bledsoe said. "His brother did the boardinghouse."

Sammy blinked fast to make the lamp stop swaying. He swiped at the dribble running from his nose. Mr. Stoker's face chilled. "So you're here to tell me my life's in danger, is that it? Do you realize I hear that kind of rumor twice a day?" He came into the edge of the light, but backed away. "Well? Let's have your version."

He had thinning hair above a wide, pale brow. A brain full of things, Sammy thought. College, and how to run a mine, and memories, and plans for tomorrow. Bam. What did a shotgun do? Little black holes?

"Is it money you're waiting for?" Mr. Stoker asked.

"Jesus," Sammy muttered. He turned to the door, stinging with contempt, but Bledsoe lounged against it.

Mr. Stoker abruptly yanked out a watch. He said, "We've got thirty-five minutes. Get some facts out of him." He went back up the stairs.

I don't want to save you, Sammy thought to his back.

Bledsoe smiled and put his fingers together like some dark gate closing. "You recollecting?"

"He's out there someplace with a shotgun."

"Think hard," Bledsoe said.

"That's all I know to tell you!"

They gazed at the hall. Bledsoe went over and cut a slice out of a cake on a sideboard. He handed it to Sammy. Sammy stared at it, and shook his head. Like Yankee at breakfast.

"Go on," Bledsoe coaxed. "It'll waste with them all gone."

"I was at the depot," Sammy said. "He's expecting bigger trouble, ain't he? Getting them off to somewhere safer."

"Bigger trouble." Bledsoe nodded.

"Will he leave, too?"

Bledsoe nodded again, eating the cake himself. "But in the other direction. Down to Denver to meet with the big hats they've sent from back east."

"To stop the strike?" he asked in a burst of hope.

"Oh, yes, it'll stop the strike. He going to ask the governor to send in state militia."

"What's that?"

"Soldier boys. With lots of shiny buttons and Gatling guns."

"How come you know?"

Bledsoe smiled, and put the glass dome back over the cake.

"You drive his car," Sammy said. "You his bodyguard?"

"Sometimes," Bledsoe said. "And his spy. And his persuader. Whatever he's comfortable calling me. The handyman."

Stoker came down the back stairs again, in his fur cap and coat. He carried a small leather case. "Let's move on," he said grimly. He glanced at Sammy. "Do you live up at Back Town?"

Sammy shook his head. He gestured downhill. "I'm—I stay in Pegler."

Mr. Stoker shrugged in irritation. "Then I'll take you down." He lifted a lantern from a shelf. "What a damned nuisance," he muttered, giving the lighted lantern to Bledsoe.

Bledsoe said cautiously, "It might be some advantage to go out in the dark, Mr. Stoker."

Mr. Stoker strode through the empty rooms to the front door. "Light him up," he ordered. "I can't have some idiot blowing his little brother to bits by mistake on my front doorstep."

He took Sammy's shoulders and led him out across the porch.

Twenty-four

COLD AIR hit Sammy's face. He forced his skittering legs to the top step, and peered through the snow hurtling down into Bledsoe's lifted light.

"You seem to be just another false alarm," Mr. Stoker said beside him. He pressed Sammy down the steps and into the car, out of the lantern shine.

Bledsoe cranked and cranked while Sammy clinched his fists to help. At last the car grumbled to life and they lurched down the driveway. Sammy leaned forward, trying to see into the gray gloom they were moving through. Every tree and rock became someone crouched and waiting. His heart pounded.

"So you've betrayed your brother," Mr. Stoker commented dryly. "Your kind usually stick together."

Sammy stared out through the snowy windshield. Bledsoe came to a stop. Sammy tensed, prickling with misgiving, but Bledsoe only wiped the snow away so he could see through the glass.

"Your father's a miner?" Mr. Stoker asked.

Sammy closed his eyes a moment and opened them on reality. "He's dead."

"Your mother?" Mr. Stoker asked.

"Her and the kids just come in on the train."

"Where do you live, then?" Mr. Stoker asked impatiently.

"Nowhere. I been staying with—" His frayed mind made a forgotten connection. "You know her, maybe. She knows you. Her name's Yankee Belew."

They rode along, jolting and rocking in a snowy nothingness. Mr. Stoker stared at Bledsoe's hat and turned-up collar.

"You knew her sister," Sammy said. He tried to keep his voice steady in the cold. "She died. Me and my folks was passing through the same town. When Yankee started back I come on out here with her. She brought her sister's little boy to raise."

Mr. Stoker turned in the dark to look at him. A gust of wind through the car's open sides sent flakes swirling around their heads.

"How old?" Mr. Stoker asked. He cleared his throat because the words had come out jumpy. "The boy. How old?"

"Little," Sammy said. Too little to be yours.

Mr. Stoker turned and stared at Bledsoe's big shoulders. He took off one glove and slowly pressed his forehead with his fingers as if he could smooth something aching behind the bone.

"Yankee had a brother, too," Sammy said.

"Yes," Mr. Stoker said. "I knew Mick." They jolted on.

"She said she'd make you exchange kids," Sammy said in a reckless rush. "So you'd know how it feels. So you'd change things. She'd lock you all up till you changed things."

Mr. Stoker put his glove back on. "She has Mick in her," he said.

The lights of town flickered past them. Each street-lamp stood in a glow of white flakes.

Mr. Stoker said, "Then I have Nell's sister to thank for your interest in my safety tonight."

Sammy pondered in silence. Had it been Yankee, saying nobody's just one thing? Had it been a little girl in red shoes? Maybe reasons were never just one thing, either. "It's my brother out there," he said.

"Yes. Of course." Mr. Stoker sighed. "Another one of Ekert's misguided clowns."

"He can do it," Sammy said. "He's done it. You better be scared."

"I'm angry," Mr. Stoker said coldly. "What in perdition is all this for? Your brother kills me. Bledsoe kills him. Then what? Do you revenge your brother? After several thousand years can't mankind come up with a better idea than retaliation?" He saw Sammy's startled face and said in a kinder voice, "Yes, I'm scared. I keep the fear up here in a small box." He tapped the side of his head. "All my feelings, good, bad. Closed up in a little box like Pandora's." The first saloon lights passed across his somber face. "I wonder sometimes, if I opened it and all the plagues and evils poured out, would the same thing be left in my box that was left in Pandora's."

"What was?" Sammy asked, not understanding.

"Hope," Mr. Stoker said.

Bledsoe half turned. "To the depot, Mr. Stoker?"

Mr. Stoker peered out. "Take High Street," he said. He leaned back slowly. "I knew a man who blew eighteen people to kingdom come. He's in the penitentiary now, serving a life sentence, braiding his horsehair bridles and reading his Bible. A nice little old man, all squared away with God." He studied Sammy sitting mashed small beside him. "Maybe there's always hope." He leaned forward. "The white house in the middle."

Bledsoe slowed. Sammy felt out into the darkness. How long will you hunt? he asked Tater. How much did Mr. Ekert tell you about Mr. Stoker's car and his plans for tonight?

They stopped. "What you doing?" Sammy asked.

Mr. Stoker got out of the car and looked up at a red glow coming from a second-story window in the white building. He leaned back into the car. "I'm going in here for a while. Bledsoe, while you're waiting you can take—" He turned to Sammy.

"Sammy," he gulped, thinking how solid Mr. Stoker's back must look in the lighted street.

"You can take Sammy back to Miss Belew's residence."

Bledsoe said, "You liable to miss your train, Mr. Stoker. I sure would like to see you on it."

"Yes," Mr. Stoker said. "Well." He waved the idea away. "There'll be another one at three in the morning."

Sammy scrambled out of the car. "No, I can't go yet. I still got to find him." He revolved, heavy with dread. "Don't stand out here," he begged. "Get inside."

He jerked to a stop in his circling. Something had moved in the dark space between two buildings.

Tater lumbered into the light through a dance of snow. The shotgun, assembled, hung from the crook of one arm. He lifted the other hand slowly from his side.

"Oh, Jesus," Sammy breathed, turning to stone.

Bledsoe was out of the car in an instant, grabbing inside his coat for the revolver in his shoulder holster.

With his free hand Tater gestured toward the pistol suddenly pointing at him. "I sure hope there's not no beans in the wheel, there. Because I'm empty." He held the shotgun out, butt down. "Sammy," he said in a voice that barely shook, "get away from him. He's safe without you."

Bledsoe took the shotgun out of Tater's hand, and pitched it to Mr. Stoker. He shoved Tater against a wall and tore open his coat to frisk him.

"Get your hands off of him," Sammy cried. "He don't have nothing else."

Mr. Stoker tipped the barrels and looked at the empty shell chambers. Bledsoe put the shells from Tater's pocket into his own.

"It was loaded once tonight," Tater said. "I had a bead on you at the depot. I could've killed you then."

"Why didn't you?" Mr. Stoker asked, laying the gun in on the car seat.

"I decided not to." He turned on Bledsoe, still crouched, alert. "Put that damn hog-leg up. I'm not going to kill him with my bare hands, neither." He turned back to Mr. Stoker. "What good would it've done me? I rather use you."

Mr. Stoker looked up at the snow, and moved under the little porch of the house. He beckoned them in beside him, and they stood incongruously bunched together, their shoulders as white as bird roosts. "How do you propose to use me?" he asked.

"I want a job," Tater said.

A gust of thankfulness caught Sammy up like a dust devil and sent him spinning. I don't care if you hate me, he thought. It was worth it.

Mr. Stoker stared at Tater and made a snort of scorn. "You take the cake for presumptuousness."

"I don't know what that is," Tater said. "But I can keep your damn car running."

They locked eyes for a long time. "You're a mechanic, I gather," Mr. Stoker said.

"I'll learn it," Tater said.

Mr. Stoker suddenly laughed. "My God, what an opportunistic little rat. Ready to leave the sinking ship and go with the winners."

Sammy said, "Is your side going to win?"

"Yes," Mr. Stoker said. "My side is going to win, and go on abusing its power until the union wins someday, and begins to abuse *its* power."

"I'm fast," Tater said. "I've done farm equipment. I want to start tomorrow. I want an advance on my pay."

"You're hard to believe," Mr. Stoker said.

"And call off your hunt for who done the boardinghouse."

"We got family," Sammy said. "Him and me. We got folks to feed." For the first time he dared to look directly into Tater's eyes.

Mr. Stoker smiled. "You understand what working for me would entail, don't you?" He watched while someone walked past, leaving splayed footprints in the snow. "You'd have to work with Bledsoe, too. Could you?"

Sammy took a silent breath and held it, suspended in doubt.

Tater's troubled eyes blinked a long time. Then his chin jutted out like Pap's. "I'll learn it," he said.

Mr. Stoker put his hand on the doorknob. "This will take some consideration."

"Take till noon tomorrow," Tater said with the same steadiness. "But let me know by then, because after that you might not be safe. Or your kid. Or your wife. Or your house." He glanced at Sammy. "I may not know how to picture it no other way."

"I believe you," Mr. Stoker said softly. He opened the door and went into a vestibule. He turned back. "I'll let you know when I get back from Denver tomorrow. It won't be noon. It will be late. A time I choose." He went up a staircase.

Twenty-five

BLEDSOE CLOSED THE DOOR. He smiled at the two of them, and took Tater's coat front in his fist and moved him over into the darkness between the house and its neighbor. He gave Tater a wallop that sent him crashing into a wall.

"What are you doing?" Sammy bellowed, trying to grab Bledsoe's arm.

Bledsoe caught Tater as he blundered out between the houses, and hit him again. Tater reeled backward, falling, and scooped a hole in the snow. He got up and stood with his hands at his sides.

"You big lard-gut," Sammy yelled, as Bledsoe peeled him off his arm, "fight me! I'll fight you." Bledsoe gave Tater a low jab that folded him like a pocketknife and sent him flying back in a long furrow. "Damn—*fight* him, Tater," Sammy begged. He ran to help him up.

Tater held to him a moment, swaying and coughing. "Get out of the way, Sammy."

"No!" Sammy said. "What's he trying to do?"

Bledsoe said, "We want to make sure nothing like the boardinghouse don't happen again. Ain't that right, fireball?" He knocked Tater down again. "And it's also because Mr. Stoker is going to give him that job, and we need to start even."

"He is?" Sammy gasped.

"Oh, yes. Mr. Stoker likes his type. So, if we going to be two men working together, he's going to have to earn his place."

Tater got up blindly and smeared the snow out of his eyes. "Beating me into the ground don't prove nothing about you." His voice had a sureness that Sammy had never heard before. "I know when a man's better than me. I killed a man better than me."

"Just the same," Bledsoe said mildly, "you could get braver tomorrow and try this foolishness again."

Tater took the piece of rope from his pocket. He limped out into the light and put it on the car seat by the gun. He looked back at Bledsoe. He had lost his hat and the snow fell melting into his burning hair. "I was brave tonight," he said.

Sammy felt his throat close up. He went across the sidewalk and stood by Tater.

Tater gestured toward the shotgun. "You might try getting that thing back to Mr. Ekert. I figure you're pretty much working both sides."

Bledsoe chuckled. "You and me may get along real good." He took the gun out of the car. "I might just leave it there in the house for him." He went toward the entrance, past Sammy's dumbfounded face.

"Is that Mr. Ekert's house?"

Bledsoe looked up at the red square of light. "You detoured Mr. Stoker, all of a sudden, peanut. I expect they going to be up there quite a while, making some private bargains."

"So the strike can end?" Sammy asked.

"So Mr. Ekert can tell his boys he won them a little something, and they ought to get back to work. And Mr. Stoker can tell his bosses they didn't lose a thing, and ought to get back to their partying. I guess that's called ending." He went in and closed the door.

Sammy peeped into the dark passage and found Pap's hat. He smoothed it gently with his sleeve, and handed it to Tater. They started slowly off. When he took Tater's arm, Tater said, "I can do it," with his teeth clinched on the pain.

"I know," Sammy murmured. But he held to him anyway.

They turned into a street where they made the first footprints.

"How come?" Sammy asked finally. "You backed out."

Tater stepped from a curb and his legs wobbled off in their own direction. "A lot of things. I seen you at the depot. Grabbing for that car." He guided himself with his hand against a wall. "I was standing there in the dark with the gun. And it was too much like that other night."

Sammy sniffed back a rush of thankfulness through the frosted hairs in his nose, and waited.

Tater said, "I got to thinking about him sitting there, brushing the flies off of me. When he didn't have to."

Sammy moved along at Tater's jerky pace, helping without seeming to. Sitting there, like you was worth saving, he said in his mind.

Tater said with difficulty, "So, tonight—I wanted him to be right about me."

They went on, stumbling through alleys, cutting across vacant lots.

Tater's teeth began to clack. "Can't walk for rat-ling," he shivered. "Got to sit."

"You'd get too cold," Sammy said, wondering what on earth he'd do if Tater passed out on him. "It's close, now."

"Reckon him and Pap sort of balanced out?" Ta-er asked. "Was that what Pap was trying to do for me—kind of a life for a life?"

"Maybe so," Sammy said, feeling a calm wonder. It was like Pap to fix it so they'd never know but could think so, even if it wasn't true. He wouldn't put it past Pap to have fixed it the way he had so Tater would grab up all that stubbornness and re-sentment he'd left him, and use it to pull them all out of the hole.

They passed the silent Odd Fellows Hall. At the foot of the stairs Tater pitched to his knees. "Guess what," he mumbled. "Can't make it up them things."

"You're going to," Sammy said. "Get up."

They climbed together, fused and tilting, like the days of getting Pap home and safe in bed.

Yankee sat alone in the room, holding the arms of Mick's chair in her sleep. She leaped up. Tater slid down against the wall, and sat looking at his thin wrists propped out on his knees. Yankee's drawn face turned to Sammy. He smiled.

Something with onions in it was staying warm on top of the stove. He looked around.

"They're up there," she said softly. "They were all so tired—the little ones—" Her eyes searched his, hurting to know.

"It's all right," he said. He looked at the five gnawed-to-nothing apple cores on a plate.

"Is he hurt bad?" she asked, staring at the bruises coloring Tater's cheek and jaw.

"He's not deaf. You can ask him," Sammy said.

She flushed so red he went on more patiently, "Sure it hurts. He got worked over pretty hard."

She brought a basin of water with a rag in it to Tater. "Wash," she said. "You've got a bloody mouth."

Tater squeezed the rag and laid his face into it.

She didn't ask anything more, but the anxiety faded from her eyes. She said with a little giggle of relief, "You both look like you stepped in front of a train."

Sammy smiled back at her, and warmed his frozen fingers on his lips. "We think Tater's got a job." He hesitated. "It's working for Mr. Stoker." He went on hurriedly, protective, "But if they'll just settle their differences we'll all be doing the same thing, won't we? Bringing out coal? Some with the money and some with the sweat."

She said, "We tried changing sides, too, Sammy, you and I. It's all right. I'm glad."

He said, "Mr. Stoker says the strike's going to end."

"Does he?" Her fingers drifted along the edge of Mick's desk.

He was sorry, too. But with the miners back at work, not so many of their wives and kids would be scrabbling for jobs. The town would come to life again, and need good workers.

He wanted to say, to ease the pain in her eyes, I'll try to make up for Mick. So all those things he was won't stop. But she was going to see to that.

She untied Pap's bedroll, and laid it flat between Tater and the stove. "Get warmer," she said. The roll had been wrapped around Pap's lariat. She lifted it, coiled tight. "Your mother said your daddy left a note scratched on the wall. He wanted you to have this."

Tater took it stiffly, smoothing the strong old hardlaid Manila strands meant to last longer than a man. After a while he said, "Is this all? Didn't he say nothing else?"

"He said, 'I'm sorry.' "

She ladled soup for them. Sammy looked up at the trapdoor, closed so kids wouldn't come falling down on them. "Is she all right, do you think?"

Yankee nodded. "It takes time." She brought a heel of bread from the wardrobe. "The rest of her things are still at the depot. She didn't know—" She broke the bread into two pieces so skimpy that she sagged in weariness. "When you go to get them tomorrow, Sammy, will you take the rest of Mick's clothes to the secondhand place?"

"Sure thing," he said softly. Mick's empty room would look different, he thought, filled with the new clutter of their belongings. He saw her face suddenly change. He looked around. Tater was crying. Soup was sloshing down his hand as his shoulders wrenched.

Yankee took the bowl from him and set it on the desk, but his freed hands reached out and held to the folds of her skirt. She hesitated, then knelt beside him, and let him put his muddy arms around her.

"Oh, God," he shuddered, "I'm sorry, too. I didn't understand."

Sammy watched her lift her uncertain arms and hold him, the way she held Charlie, because someone was supposed to.

He turned away, feeling a sting in his secret heart. He knew what to call it now. He had thought it was jealousy, but it wasn't. It was something better. And he knew with a surge of trust that it could open up like Pap's tough old ketch rope she was kneeling on, and encircle them all.

He lit another lamp and climbed the ladder one-handed. Shielding the light with his hand, he looked down on all the tired, unguarded sleeping faces.

Reba sat up beside her mother. "There's room over here, Sammy," she whispered.

"Just a minute," he whispered back. He slowly unwrapped a little bundle near his mother's head. Carefully and triumphantly he set the London Dairy teapot in the high window where it would be the first thing his mother saw against the light when she woke up.

You said, *I decided,* he reminded her, looking down at her closed eyelids, proud for her.

The little ones and Jesse were crossways on the other mattress, head to toe, with Charlie in the middle.

He heard Yankee speak, down in the room, in almost a whisper, questioning gently, and then Tater's voice, still raw but quieter, answering in a slow, halting pour of words.

He closed the trapdoor and turned out the lamp. He shucked his wet shoes and crawled in beside Reba, trying to lie small along the edge. His mother's hand reached over Reba to feel if he was covered. He couldn't tell if she did it in her sleep or in a flicker of wakefulness, thinking it was Pap like other times, coming home repentant from his fall, but she murmured, "Rest, now," and left her hand on him.

ABOUT THE AUTHOR

OUIDA SEBESTYEN had aspired to a career in writing since she was six years old. But, unable to spend the necessary amount of time required to learn her art, she wrote in "terribly earnest spurts which resulted in discouraging rejections. Four unsold adult novels and 50 unsold adult stories later, I decided I was writing for the wrong-sized people. When *Words by Heart* came pouring out, I felt I had found my niche." *Words by Heart* grew out of the author's familiarity with the West and her own family's struggle against hardship. While the work is fiction, Ms. Sebestyen adds that she drew upon stories of her parents and grandparents for a feel of the time. "Their struggles in a tiny Texas community helped shape the book. My aunt joined in supporting the family at 13, and saw all seven children through college. She, more than anyone, suggested the heroine." Quite coincidentally, that heroine was born in the same year as Ouida Sebestyen's mother. "After that, when I was uncertain about school lunches or girls wearing black stockings back in 1910, I just yelled into the kitchen and she'd yell back answers. I discovered that each question triggered enough of my mother's memories for another book." Ouida Sebestyen lives with her teenage son and her mother in Boulder, Colorado.